HAMBURGER HILL

A novel by
WILLIAM PELFREY
based on the screenplay by
JIM CARABATSOS

AVON
PUBLISHERS OF BARD, CAMELOT, DISCUS AND FLARE BOOKS

HAMBURGER HILL is an original publication of Avon Books. This work has never before appeared in book form. This is a work of fiction, and while some portions of this novel deal with historic occurrences, actual events, and real people, both living and dead, it should in no way be construed as being factual.

AVON BOOKS
A division of
The Hearst Corporation
105 Madison Avenue
New York, New York 10016

First Avon Printing: August 1987

AVON TRADEMARK REG. U.S. PAT. OFF. AND IN OTHER COUNTRIES, MARCA REGISTRADA, HECHO EN U.S.A.

Printed in the U.S.A.

K-R 10 9 8 7 6 5 4 3 2 1

This story is dedicated to the best of a
generation, the men who were at places
no different from Hamburger Hill:
Hill 881 . . . the Street Without Joy . . .
Con Thien . . . Du Bop . . . Ia Drang Valley . . .
Hue . . . LZ Jamie . . . Quan Loi . . .
Pleiku . . . the Rockpile . . . and all of the
other trails, LZs and checkpoints . . .
places forgotten, except by those
who were there.

HAMBURGER HILL

Prologue

The winter sun burned as bright and sharp as the edge of a fresh fragment of shrapnel as the Frantz family approached the long V-shaped wall. From their angle, the wall's black marble shined as brightly and harshly as the sun itself.

For Terry Frantz, the fortyish father, the endless neat columns of names etched into the marble only heightened the glare. There were some 58,000 names in all, with a few more yet to be added, arranged by year of death rather than alphabetically. A huge book had been mounted to a pedestal at each end of the V, like a Bible at the pulpit of a chapel, with the complete alphabetical listing to help people find the exact location of names.

As he led his family closer to their own reflections, Terry Frantz scanned the terrain the way he would have fifteen years ago. The black wall itself was carved into a soft grass hill. It rose from ground level at the ends and reached an apex twenty feet above the narrow concrete walk where pilgrims knelt and leaned forward to touch it. The hill served as camouflage and defilade cover from the city traffic on the other side but also seemed to shelter and intensify the emotion being released along the narrow walk.

1

A hundred feet to Frantz's rear were bronze statues of three grunts—two white riflemen and a black, "blood," machine gunner. The figures had the same tense, piercing, yet unfathomable gaze that Terry Frantz knew had now returned to his own face: the gaze of Open Grave eyes.

Letting loose his two children's hands, he made note of the differing expressions among all the pilgrims already at the wall. All of them reacted in their own unique way upon confronting their own soul in the dignified cold letters. Some—men as well as women—collapsed into tears. Others stared even more blankly than the three statues.

Frantz studied the expressions the way he had those of each new member of 3rd Squad, 1st Platoon, Bravo Company, so many lifetimes ago. He had learned quickly to size up every replacement troop's potential from nothing more than the way the guy walked and the way his eyes reacted to the bizarre world into which he had just been dropped. The ones who gazed quickly and intently would probably make it unless taken out by the fluke of a mortar round or rocket, against which everyone relied only on luck. Those who darted around bug-eyed, however, were anybody's guess. You didn't want them on point or near the radio for at least a month, if they lasted that long.

All of that, however, was too many lifetimes ago to mean anything, Terry Frantz now told himself. Too many lifetimes to count.

What are you doing, going back? he asked himself. You've put it behind you. Why did you force yourself to *come* here? It's only a block of marble. You're only another tourist.

But Terry Frantz, like most others at the wall, was far more than a tourist. Most had come not because it was on the sight-seeing map but because of the irresistible magnetism of that special name waiting somewhere to be touched.

During his own fifteen years of silently carrying the baggage, Terry Frantz had managed to convince himself that Vietnam had indeed been several lifetimes ago. He had become a different person, a solid middle-class husband and father. He had had no trouble keeping the memories strapped down deep in the back of his mind. Or so all his neighbors thought. Now, scanning the reflections of other faces along with the seemingly random names, he felt the straps stretching and breaking. The old life, the old friends, and the old pride, as well as the horror, were returning with savage chills.

His wife dropped back, again sensing what was going on in his mind. She knew better than to ask about that other life, even though she longed desperately to pull it out of him each time his eyes went blank, as they had now. He could be drinking coffee in the kitchen, watching the eleven o'clock news in the bedroom or wrestling with the children in the family room, when the eyes would suddenly glaze. He would continue whatever routine he was performing but even the children knew he had taken off to another world.

She had been surprised that he even agreed to stop at the Vietnam Veterans' Memorial today. It was a weekend excursion, they had been on their way to the Washington Monument and had no time to waste. The children had been against it, they wanted to get to the top of the monument, but Terry had uncharacteristically insisted they follow their mother's suggestion.

Now, watching him approach the stark wall, both mother and children knew Daddy had taken off again. This time, however, mother felt herself taking off with him. Clenching one of the children's hands in each of hers, she hoped that this time they could both return together. She hoped Terry Frantz the solid middle-class bread-winner would finally find a proper place for Staff Sergeant Terry Frantz the Screaming Eagle rifle squad leader and survivor of a place called Hill 937.

Five-year-old Terry, named after Daddy and dressed in her Sunday-best skirt and white knee socks, tugged impatiently at her mother's hand as she watched the reflection of Daddy's searching eyes. She tugged to go with him but Mommy pulled her back sternly.

Nine-year-old Vincent, dressed like his father in gray slacks and a wool blazer, was not as shy as Terry. Feisty Vincent had no qualms whatsoever about expressing his impatience with the whole boring scene. "Ma, how much longer?" he demanded to know.

"Just a minute, Vincent."

"Why do we have to come here?" continued the boy. When he looked up to his mother's face, however, his impatience quickly faded to fear. His mother's eyes were as blank as Daddy's got when he took off.

Little Vincent and his sister Terry were alone.

"Maybe someday he'll tell us," mumbled the mother, directing the words to the wall rather than her son as her husband fell to one knee.

He had found what he was looking for, she knew. He was kneeling like a football player called from the field to the sideline, but the game replaying itself in his mind was not football.

The graying paratroop heard none of his wife and children's distant words. The neat stone letters had taken him back to the Ashau Valley, back to May of 1969 and the 3rd Brigade, 101st Airborne Division; to a year and a world galaxies away from his family, the tourists, the civilian jetliners roaring over the distant Lincoln Memorial.

The words he now heard were not his family's or the other pilgrims' but those of the calm radio-telephone operators who were the umbilical cord between the troops in the bush, the helicopters that might or might not take them out, and the officers monitoring their casualties and kills back at battalion, brigade, and division command posts.

"Red One, Little Bear, commo check, over."

"Lazy crazy, how me."

"Same-same, thank you much, out."

Little Terry had pulled away from her mother and was pointing at Daddy but he did not see her reflection. He was lost in the reflection of his own searching eyes.

"Red Two, commo."

"Little Bear, Three, I got little people to my front, over."

"Red Three, say again."

"This is Red Three, I got beaucoup *movement two-five mikes to my front."*

"Roger that."

Terry's skirt bounced at her legs as she ran back to Mommy. "Mommy, Mommy," she called plaintively.

"Yes?" The mother still did not look down at her daughter or her son as she answered.

"Little Bear, Red One, they're in the wire, get us some sunshine, over."

"Cold Steel, fire mission, over."

"Mommy," Terry whispered intently, "Daddy's crying."

"Frantz, get your people off that bunker."

"We got wounded down there."

"Goddammit, I know that. Now lay the goddam max across the goddam bunker line."

"Get me a medic at Bravo Six."

"Chieu Hoi my ass, kill the little bastard."

Terry Frantz the husband and father was again Terry Frantz the grunt; again Staff Sergeant Terry Frantz the survivor and back bone of 3rd Squad, 1st Platoon, 3rd Battalion, 187th Infantry. He and his buddies were again firing savagely into the impenetrable triple canopy jungle from a nameless impromptu landing zone somewhere in the bowels of the Ashau Valley.

The humming of the unseen street traffic had become the dull, almost soft *thump-thump* of a barrage of NVA .60 millimeter mortar rounds leaving their steel tubes. The crisp winter cold had become soaking jungle heat as everyone waited for the incoming rounds to hit and explode. The tourists' whispering before the memorial had blurred into the staccato crack of M16 rifles with their fire selection switches flipped to automatic: "rock and roll."

The M16s drowned out the higher-pitched *crack-crack* of the enemy's AK-47 assault rifles. The nauseating whistle of incoming B-40 RPGs, rocket-propelled grenades, in turn drowned out the mortar rounds. The yelling and cursing of young men trying to unjam rifles and regroup and get help from the radio froze Terry Frantz's vocal cords but finally released the well of tears that had been dammed up for so many lifetimes.

Chapter One

The sweating, ragged, bloodied, and muddied troops of 3rd Squad, 1st Platoon, were fighting for their lives. None of them had seen an enemy face since the initial contact eight minutes ago, yet none of them even thought of how many there were or how much fire support would be needed from the distant artillery battery and the hovering helicopter gunships before they finally withdrew. Each man was totally and professionally immersed in his own small but vital task, with no time to muse on the bigger picture.

One medevac chopper had already touched down despite the continuing enemy fire and was very anxious to lift off again. The opaque green visors and oversized helmets that covered the pilot and copilot's heads hid the mixture of irrational courage and fear written all over their faces. They were hovering in the direct field of fire of the NVA's streaking green tracer rounds but could not hear either the rifles' firing or the *ping* of the bullets hitting the fuselage. All they could hear was the shrill whining of their own bird's jet turbine and the frantic calls coming from the embattled grunts' radio. The door gunners stood crouched, unprotected and defiant, blazing away methodically into the tree line with their M60 machine guns. The M60s sent out red tracers rather than green.

The birds' rotors were whipping dirt and shreds of bloodied clothing and torn C ration cartons into the backs and necks of the troops lying in the elephant grass below. The grunts didn't notice the chafing, however. They had just loaded the last body onto the bird's wide corrugated metal floor and were now silently praying that another bird would be able to come in. If another bird couldn't get in, the remaining men of 3rd Squad knew they would never get out. That was the bigger picture.

When the faceless pilot finally dipped the bird's nose and increased the seering whine of the turbine to lift off, Terry Frantz craned his neck to check the squad's defensive perimeter. He had to keep the perimeter tight; had to make sure that the gaps left by any new casualties were quickly filled and that the ammunition was distributed evenly among the men.

As usual, the troops were throwing out a constant and heavy stream of fire. As usual, the noise was too much for any of them to hear even the loudest yell. Hand signals were the normal means of communication in such situations, but today Frantz would have had to use hand signals even if the firing were to stop and the parrots, lizards, and monkeys resumed their chattering.

Frantz could not have spoken no matter how hard he tried. He had taken only a glancing round in the forehead but to keep the blood out of his eyes, Doc had rigged a crisscrossing bandage that froze his entire face. The principal ring of blood-soaked gauze went around the top of his head, covering his face from eyebrows to hairline, but the medic had placed a second one vertically, taping it at the bottom of

Frantz's chin and the crown of his head to keep the horizontal one secure.

Frantz felt like one of those characters in the silent comedy movies who always emerged from a fight with the wife with the same exaggerated crisscrossing bandage. He felt even more ridiculous with the copper-wired medical tag dangling from his fatigue jacket. Doc had wired the tag, with his blood type and a cryptic description of the wound and the time it had been incurred, to the second buttonhole of his blood-soaked baggy fatigue jacket.

There was little time to dwell on what he might look like to people back in the World, however. With the medevac helicopter target gone, the NVA regulars had now stopped firing and were regrouping behind the tree line. Frantz was the first to realize it, but was able to get his own men to cease fire only by the most frantic, chickenlike downward arm movements. After a few hand slaps against a few steel pot helmets for dramatic effect, the entire perimeter became eerily silent. Each man in the line squinted and cocked his ears trying to pinpoint enemy movement.

The silence was finally shattered by the solid, heavy sound of Duffy starting to work out with his big M60 machine gun. The muscular machine gunner had lifted the forty-pound weapon as if it were a toy and planted its bipod barrel support stand a foot farther to the left. The makeshift necklace he had made from discarded grenade pull rings, in the shape of a peace sign, danced from his chest as his shoulder vibrated against the steady slamming of the weapon.

Without moving his finger from the trigger as everyone else joined the firing, Duffy nudged his assistant gunner, Gaigin.

Skinny Gaigin, lying intently at Duffy's side, ready to take the weapon should the big gunner buy the farm, immediately understood the nudge. He ran his hand across his black Screaming Eagles neckerchief for luck before removing the last belt of ammunition draped across his chest.

"Where are they?" screamed Duffy as he paused for Gaigin to insert the new belt of ammunition into his pig. It was just a machine gun to civilians and reporters, but to the grunts who had to feed it and hump it—and who depended on it more than any other single piece of equipment save the PRC-25 radio, which was their umbilical cord to Higher—the M60 was fondly called pig.

"Where are they?" repeated Duffy.

"Out there!" yelled Gaigin as he slapped his buddy's helmet to signal that he was loaded and ready to resume fire. "Out there, out there!"

To the frantic machine gun team's immediate right, a black rifleman was fumbling desperately to unjam his M16 rifle. Motown, who casually professed to be the coolest, mellowest, and baddest of all the bloods in 1st Platoon, was in even more of a panic than the machine gunner. He could not fire and could not clear the round that had jammed itself into the chamber when the rifle had double-fed. He was totally helpless, totally vulnerable. Unlike anyone else, he was unable to divert his mind from his vulnerability through the ritualistic act of firing blindly into the tree line. If you were able to fire, even if at nothing, you were at least *doing* something.

Trying desperately to steady his sweating fingers as they grappled and then slipped off the smooth cartridge shell, Motown finally jerked his head and bit into the olive drab towel that he had draped around his neck, inside his collar. The towel was to catch the sweat from his face and ease the pressure of the rucksack's straps when humping.

He was still biting, still fumbling with the jammed round, when an NVA rocket-propelled grenade exploded just ten feet to his right. The grenade's explosion and concussion lifted a body and dropped it right in front of his field of fire.

Motown could not make out the face: it had landed on its stomach, the soles of the jungle boots facing him. The crotch was bleeding and there was no other movement than the flowing blood itself.

Staring helplessly at the crotch, Motown bit clean through the towel. Then, as he spat out the dry salty cotton, he noticed the grenades strapped to the shoulder harness of the dead troop's web gear. He was suddenly calm; suddenly no longer scared, only mad.

Fighting mad, ready to stop playing and take out some of *them*.

He began one of his standard songs as he crawled toward the body: "People say I'm the life of the party / Just because I tell a joke or two."

The cool blood removed the grenades quickly and methodically. He pulled the pins with his mellowest smile, still humming, and tossed the grenades into the tree line where he knew the NVA lay. He had long ago forgotten that he had no rifle and that green cotton shreds were jammed into his teeth.

Terry Frantz was now firing his own rifle as he moved up and down the line of defense, his silent hand signals between each burst of fire more frantic than ever. He was trying to maneuver the troops into a tighter perimeter but they were obsessed with the firing frenzy Duffy had started.

Frantz wanted them tighter to be in position to board the next helicopter as soon as it came in, before its skids even touched ground. In the back of his mind, however, he knew that a tighter perimeter might not be necessary. It was far from certain that another bird would be coming. It was still a hot landing zone and the green and red tracers and yellow muzzle flashes could be seen easily from the air. Any pilot who hadn't gone completely *dinky-dau* from too many missions into too many hot LZs would not be anxious to come in for them.

Thinking about the odds, watching half the troops continue firing as the rest dragged the newest dead and wounded to the center of the perimeter, Frantz wished he could tear off the bandages and yell. Just yell, for the sheer sake of yelling, to use the adrenaline.

A bird was coming, slapping and shrieking in from the east, but suddenly pulled back in an abrupt arch and began circling. The pilot had obviously had second thoughts and was hanging back until he got some assurance that the firefight was over.

Frantz finally threw himself prone in the cool red dirt and began crawling toward the center of the perimeter, where his fellow sergeant Douglas Worcester lay talking calmly into the black plastic telephonelike handset of his radio. The flexible coiled cord that connected the handset to the PRC-25 was stretched taut. The twenty-five-pound radio was packed inside the rucksack of the RTO, Murphy.

Worcester smiled to Frantz as he pushed the button that allowed him to transmit over the handset. He held the mouthpiece close to his chin, trying to block the noise of the shooting.

"We got this LZ secured and cleared," he casually called to the nervous pilot. "Now bring that

goddam bird down and get my people *out* of here."
He winked as he tapped Murphy, signaling for him
to lean closer with the radio. He then played with
the dials atop the radio frame for nearly a minute
before finding the frequency for the Huey gunship
that had left with the last medevac bird but was still
within easy range.

"Red Baron Two-two," he called to the gunship,
known as a "hog" to the grunts. "This is Little
Bear. When I mark for identification bring your stuff
right in on my smoke." He released the button and
again winked at Frantz as he listened to the pilot's
response.

Frantz could not hear the response but was once
again reassured by Worcester's composure. The most
seasoned veteran of the group, Worcester had been
through it all too many times to count. He had come
through it all with the calm patience and determination of a professional. Even though he had been
in the Army six years, he still denied being a lifer.
All the troops knew better than to even mention the
word *lifer* in his presence.

"Roger that, Red Baron," Worcester called to the
gunship. "The little people are all over us." He then
switched back to the original evacuation chopper's
frequency. "That's an *affirm*," he told the helicopter pilot. "*Negative* contact down here. Come on in
for us, Little Bear. Out." He slapped the handset
back into Murphy's hand and grinned mischievously
at his buddy Frantz.

"I lied." He shrugged, with a wink.

The doorless Huey whose radio call sign was still
unknown to Frantz came in fast and straight. The
ship was already in the middle of the raging firefight
by the time the pilot realized he had been conned.

There was no choice but to stay and let the grunts' covering fire assist his own escape.

Both door gunners blasted away as the skids hovered uneasily above the churning dirt and debris. Half of the remaining troops of 3rd Squad, 1st Platoon, sprang to their feet to retrieve the wounded and get them into the sanctuary of the wide corrugated metal floor while the rest laid down a field of covering fire.

Worcester had not even had time to pop the red smoke grenade to guide the hog in. All he could do now was scan the carnage of the perimeter and stand by with his radio handset to call on the hog if this bird went down.

"Ashau Valley," he mumbled to the tree line, and bit his lip. He said it to himself, more as a curse than an observation.

Terry Frantz ran in a crouch to supervise the loading of the wounded, still communicating through silent hand signals. After all the wounded were aboard, he quickly scanned the impromptu landing zone one last time. He then nodded and all the able-bodied men save Worcester ran to the high metal floor.

Worcester remained in the prone, even after his RTO Murphy had boarded. Frantz waved violently for him to go first. Worcester gave in with an arrogant smile, as if condescending to allow Frantz to be the very last man aboard.

Frantz's legs were dangling in the air as the bird lifted off but there was no room to scoot farther inside. Directly behind him, Doc was examining the wounded. The black medic did not even notice the NCO's presence, let alone try to move one of the patients to make more room and perhaps save one or two of his limbs from the NVA riflemen.

The door gunners were still blazing away with their M60s but Frantz didn't even try to fire his own M16 at the tiny fading clearing. He was looking behind, mesmerized by Doc's hands.

As usual, Doc was completely absorbed in his work, ripping open plastic-sealed battle dressings and inserting needles from intravenous bottles into those troops in most urgent need. He worked in a frenzy that might have appeared haphazard to a stateside civilian but was in fact smooth, rhythmic, and thoroughly professional.

When Doc finally glanced out the doorless bay to make sure the floating bird was out of small arms range, he noticed a gash in Frantz's shoulder. He had been reaching for a sterile gauze to give another of his patients but instead gave it to Frantz. "Hold that," he commanded, in a drill sergeant voice that easily overcame the shrill grinding and whining of the helicopter's turbine and rotors. Slapping the dressing against Frantz's shoulder, he immediately turned his attention back to the more seriously wounded. He began examining their boots, looking for dog tags to identify their names and blood type.

After inserting the needle from the thin plastic tube of an intravenous bottle into one man's arm, he realized he had left himself holding the bottle. The boy he had just injected was still bleeding and others still hadn't been looked at. He *couldn't* hold the damned thing all the way back to base camp, but there was no place to hang it.

He was still searching frantically for a hook or nook when Terry Frantz reached back and took the bottle without speaking.

With no time for thanks, Doc went to work on the wounded boy whose life was now strung to the bottle in Terry Frantz's hand. "Talk to me, troop," he implored, trying to hide the gravity of the wound with the soft tone of his voice. "What's your name?"

"Lagunas," said the groggy boy, barely audible in the shrieking and vibrating helicopter. "Private First Class."

Doc leaned closer to the sweating face. "Where you from?" he asked.

"Fort Worth. Mama . . ."

"Talk to *me*," ordered Doc as he watched him fade. "To *me*." He began shaking him. "Fort Worth is a hell of a town."

"It sucks," said Pfc. Lagunas before relaxing his facial and neck muscles and dying.

Doc pounded the boy's chest savagely, going through the ritual of trying to revive him even though he knew he was gone.

Frantz looked on helplessly.

"Fucking bummer," the medic grumbled when he finally leaned back on his heels to take one deep breath before returning to the others.

"There it is," said the fellow-blood Motown, appearing from nowhere in the corner of the bird's womb.

There it is, thought Terry Frantz as he turned away to the floating blue sky. His M16 lay useless at his side, held tight by the weight of an unconscious man's thigh.

Frantz didn't even realize he still held the bottle over the dead soldier. Nor did he realize he was still pressing Doc's dressing against his own shoulder wound with his other hand. If someone had asked, he would have been unable to say how or when in the firefight he had been hit in the shoulder. He didn't even remember the head wound.

But it didn't mean anything.

Those were the thoughts and phrases that summarized every grunt's philosophy for day-to-day survival. *There it is: it don't mean nothing.*

The wind from the moving helicopter cut soothingly into the dried blood and sweat that had covered Terry Frantz's face. Beneath him, the treetops of the lush green valley looked like soft dyed cotton balls. An air strike was already being called into the area the squad had just left. The explosions sent ripples through the trees' canopy before the noise was even audible.

Frantz was suddenly tired. He wanted to close his eyes and lie back against the dead man behind him to sleep. But he couldn't release the bottle, and he couldn't close his eyes. Though only twenty years old, Staff Sergeant Terry Frantz knew that, after all his eyes had seen in less than a year in Vietnam, they would never rest again. Open Grave eyes, the troops called them.

Chapter Two

Douglas Worcester stood beside the idle two-and-a-half-ton truck with his hands on his hips and his feet spread apart. That was the standard pose all noncommissioned officers assumed when reviewing a new area of operation or a new group of recruits. This morning, however, it was safe and familiar terrain and he was not reviewing new recruits—not yet. He was merely passing the time, eyeballing the variety of other vehicles passing by on the red dirt road.

The pose had become reflex. The passing traffic was the usual array of passing jeeps, other deuce-and-a-halfs and occasional tracked armored personnel carriers.

Above Worcester's shoulder, the four newest men assigned to Bravo Company sat uneasily in the sand-bag-lined bed of the deuce-and-a-half. Thoroughly intimidated by the platoon sergeant's very presence, they dared not speak, even among themselves. They were straight from the World. FNGs: fucking new guys.

Worcester did not have to turn and look up to visualize the innocent youth and naïveté on their faces. He knew his own face and Terry Frantz's had also been innocent once, but did not want to picture or remember it.

The four FNGs sat atop their new rucksacks with their rifles resting clumsily across their laps. Their clothes and gear were the same as Worcester's but looked centuries newer, as did their faces. They all had shiny new stitched name patches above the top of the right breast pocket.

Beletsky and Bienstock were white. Beletsky looked far younger than his nineteen years and Bienstock was lost in his green jungle fatigues and huge steel pot helmet.

Galvan, a Chicano from Albuquerque, New Mexico, scanned his comrades and the passing traffic with the intensity that showed the potential makings of a good soldier.

The fourth man, Washburn, was a soul brother from Georgia who looked even more lost than Beletsky and Bienstock.

All four were watching the one other FNG who would be going forward with them that morning, Vincent Languilli. Languilli had boldly declined to mount the truck with them. He had wanted to take advantage of the last opportunity to get his rocks off before going forward, despite all the base camp NCO's lectures against doing it with the unregistered locals. He was now standing at a Pepsi machine, a few feet back from the parked deuce-and-a-half, talking to his two new Vietnamese girl friends.

Handsome Vinnie Languilli, as full of life as he would have been on a corner back in the World, had the girls giggling as he pulled two matchbooks from his fatigue jacket.

"Come on, girls-san. Tell me how you say that again."

One of the girls held Languilli's hand and pointed to his watch. "You souvenir me this, I tell you. You number one."

Languilli tried again. "*Beaucoup dao tiem. La de* . . . something-something. That's right, isn't it?"

"You speak Vietnamese number ten thousand, Ligoolo," giggled the first girl.

"Languilli," he corrected her. "Languilli." He was still smiling at her when he heard the platoon sergeant calling him.

"Your dick will fall off if you get any closer to that pussy, troop," called Worcester, with his hands still on his hips. "They'll keep you in the Philippines with the black VD and you'll never go home. Get back in the truck."

Vinnie Languilli stared hard at the lifer's cold emotionless face as he obeyed.

Worcester's attention had already shifted from the FNG to a jeep speeding toward them. It stopped beside the deuce-and-a-half with a shearing squeal.

"My, my. I thought you bought a water buffalo and your own rice paddy to shit in!" cried Worcester as Terry Frantz leaped from the passenger side of the vehicle. "Where the hell have you been, Young Stuff?"

"Surfing," said Frantz, with a broad, teasing, shit-eating grin.

The deuce-and-a-half driver was already revving up his engine. The two veterans slapped each other's shoulders and then scampered quickly up into the back of the truck. The truck bed was lined with sandbags for protection against mines that might be planted in the road. The five new replacement troops sat nervously before the cases of C-rations, beer, soda, and other supplies crammed toward the cab of the truck; still too intimidated to speak.

Frantz wrapped a piece of black plastic around the muzzle of his M16 as soon as he sat down. The plastic cap would not interfere with firing but would keep dirt and other debris out of the barrel.

Watching him, the five FNGs quietly pulled the muzzle caps they had been issued by the company armorer from their leg pockets and mimicked the veteran.

Frantz then proceeded to tape an extra magazine to the one already in his weapon. He taped the new one upside down, so he could reload the rifle in a single quick motion rather than fumble with a bandolier or an ammo pouch.

Four of the five FNGs chose not to follow this particular old-timer's trick. They didn't have any tape and they didn't want to look any more self-conscious than they already were by asking for the sergeant's. The fifth, however, Galvan the strong-eyed Chicano, produced a roll of tape from his fatigue jacket and copied Frantz's movement meticulously and naturally.

"I was at the hospital in Cam Ranh," Frantz was telling Worcester. "They made me NCO in charge of burning feces in an orderly, proficient, military manner. So I took a walk." A boyish grin swept across his face. "I met a nurse."

"No," said Worcester.

"Round-eye," Frantz said, nodding.

"You didn't," repeated the grinning older platoon sergeant.

"She had her own trailer, on the beach."

"No."

Frantz nodded proudly. "I figured, what can they do to me? Send me to Vietnam? I moved in with her. The Mamas and Papas found me on the beach.''

Worcester's grin broadened. Mamas and Papas: Military Police. "Surfing?'' he asked his friend.

"Are you kidding?'' Terry Frantz gloated. His head wound back at the last firefight, when Doc had bandaged his jaw closed, had turned out to be the best thing to happen since leaving the World. The nurse had not been beautiful and her face was already fading from memory with the imminent return to the boondocks, but she had been less inhibited than even a Vietnamese prostitute. Terry Frantz had never slept with an American girl before and had made a secret promise to always remember her name.

Worcester replied to the teasing question by turning to the five FNGs as if he hadn't even noticed their disgusting presence until now. He pointed to the heavy flak jackets curled over their shoulders.

"What are you wearing that shit for?'' he demanded. "It's just going to dehydrate your ass and don't do you any good.''

"But, Sarge,'' begged Beletsky in a trembling and worried voice, "they told us at Division training to—''

"We had a short-timer once,'' Worcester interrupted. "Johnny-I-Forget-His-Name. *He* wore a flak jacket, two helmets, and armor underwear.'' He made the motion of masturbating, one of those universal gestures that could summarize any one of a dozen different situations or emotions in the infantryman's world. "Ashau Valley.'' He shrugged. "If your time's up, your time's up.''

"What's the Ashau Valley?'' asked young Beletsky, not noticing the hardening in Terry Frantz's face as the veteran forgot his nurse's first name.

Chapter Three

The dust-coated deuce-and-a-half carrying Frantz, Worcester, and the five FNGs assigned to 1st Platoon, Bravo Company, rolled north on a smooth winding asphalt highway. The road seemed out of place with the wild mountains and their deceptively soft and lush-looking triple canopy jungle. It could have been a two-lane country highway anywhere back in the World, except for the patches of darker and newer asphalt that covered mine craters rather than potholes.

And except for the occasional armored personnel carriers stationed along it every mile or so. The APCs had cyclone fence strung around them to detonate incoming rockets and grenades before they could hit the vehicles.

The truck finally began slowing as it approached a bridge. The FNGs craned their necks to the activity ahead.

The bridge spanned the thin An Lo River. At this point, the river had settled into a wide, deep ravine. Fighting bunkers had been built at each end of the skeletal steel-frame bridge, with .50 caliber machine guns mounted atop the sandbag roofs. The guards' rifles, bandoliers, and grenades were placed neatly beside the machine guns, ready for action.

The lounging guards did not bother to wave at the deuce-and-a-half.

The FNGs' eyes had already shifted from the bunkers and terrain to the Vietnamese civilians washing clothes and peddling Pepsis to the other GIs lounging by the water's edge. Beletsky, Washburn, Galvan, and Bienstock scanned the entire scene with anxious curiosity but Vincent Languilli's gaze froze immediately on a young Vietnamese woman washing her hair. She stood knee-deep in the water, with her black *au-dai* slacks rolled up and the long loose blouse that would normally have flowed to her knees tucked loosely at her waist. Her long black hair glowed and the water drops sparkled as she bent and shook her head to rinse it.

The truck slowed to a crawl at the other side of the bridge, at the edge of a village situated before an immaculately diked rice field and the distant bluish cloud-covered mountains. The deuce-and-a-half continued past several more APCs ringing the village and finally stopped before an apparently abandoned temple. The temple was pockmarked with bullet holes. Huge chunks of paint and plaster had been knocked out at the corners and beneath the windows. On closer inspection, however, it was very much inhabited. Improvised clotheslines had been strung beside it, heavy with olive drab fatigues and socks. The ground was littered with unopened cases of ammunition and C-rations. A thick twenty-foot-high "292" radio antenna rose from a rear corner.

The original Buddhist sanctuary had been converted to the current command post for Bravo Company, 3rd Battalion, 187th Infantry.

The arriving FNGs were more impressed with the relaxed attitude of the troops strolling near the CP than with the bizarre use of the temple itself. The

troops were openly fraternizing with Vietnamese civilians, joking and playing with the children and
bickering with the old near-toothless mama-sans over
trinkets in an improvised open market area within a
grenade's throw of the command post.

The FNGs climbed down from the high truck
without being told to, straddling the bed's wooden
slat railing and then stepping on the tire before awkwardly jumping to the ground with their new rucksacks and loose steel pots still on. They all fell on
their faces under the weight. Frantz and Worcester
watched them with the disdain of seasoned professionals.

"I'm going to put the new people in your squad,"
said Worcester.

"Oh shit," replied Frantz, with a resigned groan
that was part protest but also a fatalistic acceptance
of what he had known would happen all along.
Third Squad had been decimated in the last ambush,
when he himself had received the gashes that had in
turn given him the brief respite of a week at the field
hospital and a few nights with the round-eye nurse
whose name he could no longer remember. Third
Squad was always a choice grinder for new meat.

"Don't 'oh shit' me, troop. The old man has *me*
breaking in another new lieutenant. He looks like
Palmolive fucking soap."

"I don't need this FNG shit, Worcester," declared Frantz as he watched the awkward replacement troops play with their ruck straps and steel
pots. The innocent nervous faces made him nauseous.

Worcester only smiled cruelly. "Yeah, well you
write your Congressman and tell him I 'need' a
steak," he said. "And a bucket of cold beer and a
round-eye to wrap a leg around."

Frantz finally shut up as he watched Worcester turn and walk toward the new lieutenant. He knew that Worcester was sympathetic. The cruel grin was a professional gesture. Worcester now had his own problems.

The lieutenant looked even greener and more lost than the FNG enlisted men. His new uniform was spotless and starched; his canvas-topped jungle boots were polished, the trousers tucked and bloused perfectly at the top. The black stitching of the stiff name tag above his right breast pocket stood out like a neon sign: EDEN.

Lieutenant Eden, obviously fresh from Officer Candidate School at Fort Benning, Georgia, couldn't have been in Vietnam more than ten days. Worcester was right, thought Frantz as he watched the veteran platoon sergeant approach his new ward. He really does look like Palmolive fucking soap.

After explaining where 3rd Squad's sector of the defense perimeter began and ended, Frantz led his five FNGs to a sleeping bunker and told them to dump their fighting gear on the sandbag roof. Before they could even glance inside the underground dirt cubicle that was their new home, however, he told them to grab their rifles and a bandolier of ammunition and follow him. He then took them to the farthest edge of 1st Platoon's sector of the perimeter. One of the bunkers had lost part of its top layer of sandbags to a mortar round, and the C.O. also wanted some more wire in front of all bunkers on the line as further protection against sappers.

Neither the sandbags nor the wire would make much difference in the end if the enemy decided he really wanted to take this one insignificant village fire base, but the assignment was a good way to get the FNGs accustomed to the monotony and drudgery of fire-base life right away.

Frantz assigned Bienstock, from Queens, and the soft-spoken black Georgian, Washburn, to fill sandbags for reinforcing the bunker. He then ordered Beletsky, Galvan, and Languilli to start stringing new concertina wire in front of the bunker.

The coiled wire's razor-sharp points quickly cut into the stringers' hands but they dared not show any emotion. Staff Sergeant Frantz was still there, with his hands on his hips.

Frantz studied each man carefully. It was immediately obvious that Galvan, the Chicano who had mimicked him in taping a second magazine beneath his M16's breech, was the best of the bunch. Galvan worked methodically and soon had the others imitating him without having to speak to them.

"What did they say the signal was for incoming rounds?" asked Beletsky.

"I can't tell the difference between incoming and outgoing," volunteered Bienstock. "I dived off the shitter at Camp Evans and it was just our stuff going out."

"I think it's two long sirens," said Beletsky, answering his own question.

Vinnie Languilli paused from his wire stringing to call over to Beletsky. "Don't worry about it!"

"I'm not worrying. I just think that it's important to know the signal for incoming rounds."

Ignoring him, Languilli knelt to fill two empty tin cans with pebbles. He then carefully lodged the cans in the tightly coiled wire and shook them. They rattled loudly.

"Don't worry. Nobody's getting in here tonight," he boasted.

"What's the signal for ground attack?" asked Beletsky, as if he had never been interrupted.

"Three short ones," answered Bienstock confidently.

"Green star cluster," said Galvan, breaking his silence to correct the New Yorker.

"That's great for night, but what about day?" asked Beletsky.

Languilli straightened and held his aching lower back. "Birdshit and paratroopers are the only things that fall out of the sky," he told Beletsky. "Hey, Sarge," he called over to Frantz, who was calmly taking it all in, "are there any women around here?"

Frantz did not reply.

"Hey, man, I'm not screwing any whore," volunteered Beletsky.

"Shit," grumbled Washburn.

Languilli flashed a teasing smile to the sweating black troop. "You'd eat her pussy."

"If you can't fry it, I don't eat it," said Washburn in his deep but mild Georgia drawl.

"A year is a long time," lamented Bienstock.

Beletsky straightened to pull a picture from his wallet. "That's Claire," he said proudly.

Languilli stepped closer to examine the snapshot. "If she's fucking for peace," he said, "I'm on the wrong side."

Languilli was still grinning as Beletsky swung on him. It was an awkward right hook and missed but Languilli tripped on the concertina wire as he stepped aside. The jiggling of the wire set off one of the flares that had been set for unwelcome night visitors.

Galvan, the cold Chicano, was quickly between the two of them, wordlessly breaking it up before either man could throw another punch.

"I'm *marrying* her, man," growled Beletsky, with nostrils flaring and fists still clenched; the pose of a street fighter rather than a nervous cherry replacement troop.

"I didn't mean anything," retorted Languilli, with the same street fighter's calm defiance.

Galvan again spread his arms to keep them apart. "Languilli, Beletsky, shake hands," he commanded. "We're Airborne. We don't start fights—"

Washburn lifted his chin as he interrupted to finish the paratroops' creed: "We finish 'em."

"There it is." Bienstock nodded.

Languilli finally eased back and extended his hand to Beletsky. "*Vincent* Languilli," he told him.

"*Joseph* Beletsky."

The faintest trace of a smile crept over Terry Frantz's face as he watched the inevitable bonds of friendship forming between the green troops. They had all obviously already made the subconscious realization that they were now brothers whether they liked it or not. They had to pull together to survive their 365 days, regardless of what their different lives had been just three months ago, before basic training, infantry training, jump school, and that long ride across the pond in the silver bird. They had already determined, again without realizing it, that survival would be easier if they tried to take it with pride, patience, and cooperation rather than bitterness.

The troops' mixed anxiety and pride reminded Frantz of the awkward FNG he himself had been, seventeen or so lifetimes ago.

Before any of his new team members could see his smile, however, Frantz broke away from them and went to the temple command post for a solitary coffee break. He filled an empty discarded C-ration can from a pot that had *Lifer Juice* written on it. He then moved back near the entrance and squatted unobtrusively on his heels, Vietnamese-style, to watch Lieutenant Eden brief all the new men who had arrived since his trip to Cam Ranh Bay—including the five FNGs from 3rd Squad, who had apparently been quickly rounded up by another N.C.O. The lieutenant had called a motley formation right outside the entrance of the CP and was taking the men through the motions of filling out the standard Pentagon forms that had been saved for their final assignment to a unit.

Someone's civilian transistor radio was blaring in the background with the latest Armed Forces Radio news broadcast. Doc, Motown, and McDaniel, the grenadier, strolled in front of Frantz and stopped to do an improvised precision step to the tinny notes of Motown's cassette recorder, oblivious to the green Lt.'s briefing. Motown had put on a tape of Smokey Robinson's "I Second That Emotion" and the bloods were mouthing the words. Frantz again smiled at the absurd scene.

"If you do not want anyone notified in case of injury," Lieutenant Eden was saying, "check box three. Otherwise, write the name—last name first, first name last—and address on line four."

He held up a sample form and pointed to the lines as the Armed Forces Radio's base camp commando disc jockey read the news. Terry Frantz cringed at the smooth baritone radio voice. The disc jockey was undoubtedly a Spec 4 who slept in a bed every night and had never even thought about what it would be like to have the straps of an eighty-pound rucksack cut into his shoulders while he tried to crawl up a mud slope infested with leeches and centipedes without being able to wipe the burning sweat from his eyes or even think about beds or nontactical radio transmissions.

"There has been another delay in the Paris peace negotiations due to a seating disagreement," the baritone was saying as the three bloods whirled to Smokey Robinson's mellow notes and Lieutenant Eden continued his briefing.

"Line five is for your beneficiary. You have in your possession forms for Savings Bonds, Series E type. I highly recommend that you sign up for this program, men; plan for the future."

Frantz savored the bitter but piping hot coffee as he continued to take it all in with his eyes and ears. This was what Vietnam really came down to, he thought to himself. Savings Bonds and beneficiaries, Smokey Robinson music and the right seating arrangement in Paris, France. What higher values could you hope to be asked to fight for?

"The Defense Department reports that its Vietnamization and troop withdrawal plans are ahead of schedule. The fact that there are more American personnel in Vietnam this month than last is attributed to normal operating procedure."

"The white card should be filled out by married men," explained Lieutenant Eden. "It provides for joint access to your funds in case of emergency."

"This is Specialist Harris," added the disc jockey, "reminding you once again that my favorite show is on tonight. That's 'Hullabaloo,' and the girls in the cages will be dancing *especially* for all of you night fighters in the First-of-the-Ninth at Quan Loi."

Lieutenant Eden was now displaying his final form for the new arrivals. "Additionally," he said, "there is one postcard for each of you. Fill this out and advise your family that you are safe and how to get in touch with you. Mail is a priority. You do not need stamps. You can write on a piece of C-rat box, address it, and it will be delivered free of charge." He paused for a deep breath and then raised his voice. "Questions?" he asked, his voice sliding and squeaking up an octave.

The three veteran black troops were totally immersed in the lyrics and rhythm of "I Second That Emotion." They danced the way they fought, like a precision machine. They could have taken three years of lessons and had five hours of rehearsal with a New York choreographer on this one song and still not come any closer to duplicating one another's moves.

They even wore their clothes the same way, like a specialty team. Each of the three had tied a spare set of bootlaces around his calves in a crisscrossing pattern, making the baggy green jungle fatigues billow out from his thighs like balloons. Each also had a rolled green towel around his neck, tucked under the collar like an ascot, and a bracelet on the left hand made from the black plastic-coated wires used to tie sandbags—the same kind of wires that tied garbage bags and bread bags back in the World.

"Brother blood!" called Doc at the conclusion of the song, smiling at the scar on Frantz's forehead.

Frantz finally rose from the Vietnamese squat and enthusiastically joined the brothers, mimicking their jaunty walk, with his hands in his pockets. Each of the three black troops gave him the intricate ritual handshake normally reserved only for fellow bloods—the "dap," the universal gesture of broth-

erhood. The dap was a special show of both pride
and defiance, reserved for the group whose presence
in combat units was so far disproportionate to their
presence in the general public back in the World;
that proud group who had an even tougher time
trying to rationalize being where they were than did
the other grunts. The dap was just one of many special ways they had of communicating their pride and
strength against the honkies' childish self-pity and
the lifers' even more childish speeches and missions.

"Shit, I do good work," said Doc as he continued to examine Frantz's scar.

"How's it going, Doc?" asked Frantz, with the
slightest twinge of self-consciousness.

"By hand," said Doc. He made the gesture of
jerking off; a gesture that everyone in Bravo Company by now knew was as much a part of Doc's
natural body language as the dap.

"Hey, Sarge," intervened McDaniel, who was
now one of the "shortest" men in the platoon; one
of those with the least number of days remaining on
his tour of duty. "Buzz around town is that Doc's
been on R and R." He winked and elbowed Doc in
the ribs.

"And you *are* going to tell me all the horny,
jacking-off details," commanded Frantz.

Doc drew his eyebrows. "I thought I cut that little thing off when you got hit," he said to his white
friend.

"You couldn't find it," teased the cool rifleman
Motown.

Doc finally eased up on Frantz and proceeded
with the report of his adventures on R and R, five
nights and six days away from Vietnam, Republic

of. "The girls wear numbers and you just pick one out," he reported. "Bangkok is not believable."

"Doc's going to marry one and send her home to Mama," interrupted McDaniel.

"Say what?" demanded Doc, slapping his hands against his hips in indignation.

"What happened after I got medevacked?" asked Frantz. As soon as he asked the question, however, he regretted it. He knew he had ended the playful bantering and brought all four of them back to the reality of the present absurdity.

Motown shook his head respectfully as he replied, "Mr. Chuck definitely had his shit together."

"Speedy?" asked Frantz.

"Who?" said Doc.

"The shit burner from Second Squad. Gonzales."

"Traumatic cranial contusion," reported Doc. "I couldn't ventilate him."

"Brother Jones got blown to shit," added McDaniel.

"Who's Jones?" asked Frantz.

"The FNG," answered Motown. "He knew everything the Temptations ever did. Make sure we get some *brothers* in the squad. I don't want to hear any more of that rebel"—he began singing in a hoarse mockery of all country-and-western music—"that 'I lost my car on the mother-fucking road and I'm crying over you,' shit."

The three bloods again dapped. Frantz was conscious of being deliberately excluded this time. McDaniel then again confronted him in his most serious tone.

"Hey, Sarge," he said. "I got a new flash for you. A brother I was hanging out with in Delta Company who drives Iron Raven around says rumour has it we're going back into the Ashau. I am too *short* for that shit, man. Doc won't give me a profile, maybe you can see if there's a job at headquarters for me.''

Doc's face was suddenly as cold as steel, his voice as stern as that of a judge passing sentence on a thief. ''They don't take niggers at headquarters, brother,'' he told McDaniel. ''All the white motherfuckers are back there.''

Frantz turned back to where Lieutenant Eden had been giving his briefing but everyone had dispersed. When he turned back to Doc, the squad's indispensable medic was still looking fiercely into the nervous short-timer's eyes.

Frantz decided not to argue with Doc over the remark. He wasn't even offended, let alone angered. His only concern was whether Doc was developing an attitude problem that might sometime jeopardize anyone in the squad. They had to pull together to survive, no matter what else was happening in the broader world beyond 3rd Squad; no matter what had happened to any of them before they had been thrown together; no matter what injustice might await them back in the World.

Doc meant no personal offense to Terry Frantz with his statement of the facts to McDaniel. He only wanted to remind the fellow blood of the facts of life in the man's army.

McDaniel did all bloods proud when he worked out in the bush, no honky could lay down a faster, smoother, more accurate field of fire with the M79 grenade launcher, but his ways with the man when the squad wasn't on patrol often revealed that sense of insecurity he had no doubt shown the man back in the World. Doc remembered only too well how he had felt and shown that same insecurity, and was determined never to show it again. Not after what he had been through. He had proven he could toe the line and carry the burden as well as any man of any color or income tax bracket. And he was not going to let anyone treat him any other way.

Doc ended up brooding over that brief encounter all afternoon. He truly liked Terry Frantz. You couldn't ask for anyone steadier in the bush, and you couldn't ask anyone to treat his troops fairer. Frantz's only concern was getting everybody through, which was also Doc's own concern. Doc knew that if it came down to it, each of them would have given his life for the other without the slightest hesitation. He was sad that Frantz had to be present when he reminded McDaniel of the facts of life in the man's army.

He was still brooding that evening when he called all the platoon's newest arrivals together for the required special fluoride treatment. The man's army had decided that happy and healthy troops were ones with no cavities. Tons of special tubes of extra-gritty toothpaste and extra-firm toothbrushes had been shipped to Vietnam so that each troop would be assured of at least one sound tooth cleaning before meeting whatever fate awaited him.

After issuing the tubes of toothpaste and cellophane-wrapped brushes, Doc took his command position in front of the motley column. He noticed 3rd Squad's five FNGs—Beletsky, Languilli, Washburn, Galvan, and Bienstock—standing together, apart from the rest. Spreading his feet to a drill instructor's modified parade-rest position, he concentrated his remarks on them specifically, rather than the larger group.

"Remove the protective wrapping from the toothbrush," he commanded, speaking as fast as a runaway machine gun. "Put the wrapping next to your left foot. Open the toothpaste." He paused, waiting for them all to do it. "Place the cap on top of the wrapping. Now, put a generous amount of paste on the sterile bristles. People, you will brush your teeth in a rapid vertical motion for one minute. That's up and down for you rebel mo'fuckers. When I say stop, you will turn to your right and spit. Ready! *Brush!*"

He walked up and down the line, watching them obey, with his hands folded behind his back and his neck craned in another classic drill instructor's pose. "You may notice a granular taste," he continued. "That's pumice. Its purpose is to seer the teeth and allow the fluoride to penetrate. Gentlemen, in Vietnam you *will* be confronted by many organisms in the food, water, and air that are foreign to American bodies. Ringworm, impetigo, malaria, amoebic dysentery, and crotch rot. It has been found that proper dental hygiene is an important component in maintaining a healthy fighting man."

He kept eyeballing the line as he paced and spoke, proud that they were brushing in a perfect vertical motion, the way any terrified boy would have the first night of basic training back at Fort Knox or Fort Bragg. The sense of pride and power vanished, however, when one of 3rd Squad's FNGs abruptly stopped brushing and spat all of the toothpaste out of his mouth.

"What *are* you doing?" demanded Doc.

"Lighten up, bro," said Beletsky before wiping his mouth with his sleeve.

"I'm not your 'brother,' troop. Now, did I tell you to spit?"

"No, sir."

"If you want to walk out of this fucking place you *will* listen to people who *know*. Be an 'individual' and I'll be tagging your ugly toothless face straight on its way to the long box with metal handles! Now brush your teeth in a rapid vertical motion, *troop*."

Beletsky had no idea why the crazed medic had jumped so deep in his shit. But he also knew better than to ask. This medic was obviously one soul brother who took everything he did seriously, even though he had to know just as well as everyone in the line how ludicrous the tooth-brushing routine really was. Respecting the medic's pride and poise—and fearful of the consequences of another rebuke—Pfc. Languilli resumed brushing in a rapid vertical motion with no further comment.

Chapter Four

Next morning, the sun rose softly through the heavy mist and fog that were lifting from the mountains beyond the village and its rice field. First Platoon, Bravo Company, did not stir until the troops who had drawn the last two hours of perimeter guard duty, the "graveyard shift," yelled into the sleeping bunkers to roust them. The men in each bunker responded with a mixture of hoarse coughs, curses, and thrown boots.

As usual, none of them had rested well. The intermittent firing of outgoing artillery and mortar rounds, combined with every man's obligation to pull two hours of guard duty at a different time each night (not to mention the ever-buzzing mosquitoes and flies), ensured that no one ever got far enough asleep to pose a threat of waking anyone else with his snoring.

Sleep was made even lighter and more fitful by the squeaking air mattress each man spread across the dirt ledge carved out two feet below ground level to serve as a bed. Every move, even the slightest wiggle, even a deep breath, caused the olive drab air mattress to give and squeak in another place. Added to this, each man slept fully clothed, weapon at his side, tucked into one of the grooves between

39

the air mattress's tubes of air. Each slept with his boots on one side of his head and steel pot on the other. No one ever got more than five hours' total sleep a night, max.

By the time the five FNGs of 3rd Squad stirred, Duffy, the machine gunner, and Gaigin, his assistant gunner, were already boiling water to make hot chocolate. They had punched holes in a discarded C-ration can to make a stove and dropped a blue heat tab into the can. The heat tab burned still and blue, like natural gas, and gave off so much heat that no one could pick up a canteen cup left over it more than a minute.

Murphy, Platoon Sergeant Worcester's RTO, was removing the long and heavy rectangular battery from his radio. The radio, a PRC-25, weighed twenty-five pounds; the battery, another two pounds. That weight, added to the RTO's normal battle gear and rations, more than justified all RTO's calling it a "prick-25" when they had to hump the mountains that were the 101st Airborne Division's area of operation. Murphy carefully wiped the condensation from the battery with a towel and reinserted it to make a commo check with the CP before proceeding with the rest of his morning routine.

The five FNGs, of course, still had no routine. Their clothes were already filthy compared to the way they had looked at Camp Evans but still looked new and clean next to the other troops'. Their eyes still had the glaze of innocence and self-consciousness as well as lack of sleep. They hovered together in front of their bunker, apart from everyone else. The only one who seemed to know where he was or what he was supposed to do was Galvan, the Chicano, who had emerged before the others and had already made a heat tab stove to boil some water for drinking and brushing his teeth.

"Did you sleep?" asked boyish Beletsky, scanning a row of troops who had filled their steel pots with water and were shaving. He was again addressing Vincent Languilli, the handsomest and least shy of the newcomers.

"I kept seeing things," said Languilli.

"What do you mean, you keep seeing things?"

Languilli shook his head and walked away, annoyed with Beletsky's constant game of Twenty Questions.

Beletsky then turned to Washburn, the soft-spoken Georgian. "Did you sleep?" he asked.

Washburn had only to look at him with his swollen red eyes to answer the question.

"I thought I heard something," said Bienstock, who looked even more lost in the wrinkled baggy fatigues than he had yesterday.

"This is bullshit!" said Beletsky. "We *got* to sleep. What are we going to do, stay awake for a year?"

Galvan silently rose from his C-ration stove and handed Beletsky his canteen cup, now filled with boiling hot chocolate.

Ten feet away, before another sleeping bunker, Staff Sergeant Terry Frantz was running a razor across his face. He didn't bother to use soap, lather, or a mirror; just the tepid water from his steel pot. He also did not bother to turn his gaze from the distant fog-covered blue mountains as he heard Worcester approaching on his morning rounds to check the perimeter.

"Arise!" bellowed Worcester. "Awake and salute another glorious morning, you scroungy-assed sons of bitches."

Worcester stopped at Frantz's side and offered him a sip of his steaming black coffee.

"You found a home in the army, Worcester," said Frantz.

"Same-same you, Young Stuff. Same-same." Worcester wasn't that much older than the others by the standards used back in the World—he had twenty-three years compared to their nineteen or twenty—but he had already put in six years in the army. Six years: long enough to get him two tours in Vietnam and permanent Open Grave eyes. Long enough to make him an old man and a lifer in the eyes of any FNG.

"*I'm* no lifer," said Frantz. "Forty-one and a wake-up and *fini* Vietnam, *fini* fucking green machine, I'm going to be a Private Fucking Civilian, with places to go—"

"People to see," said Worcester.

"Things to do," said Frantz, completing the vow.

Worcester's grin faded as he stared at the five replacement troops. "I want you to keep an eye on these young boys in case we have to go back to the Ashau," he told Frantz.

"They don't mean nothing," Frantz said with a shrug, the sudden dryness in his voice betraying the lie. Frantz did care, despite the facts that he was a short-timer and caring only led to grief.

Worcester cringed as Motown's cassette player blared from somewhere behind him. "Don't they ever play Tammy Wynette?" he asked.

Frantz did not hear the question. He was again lost in the nervous faces of the milling FNGs.

Two hours later, Terry Frantz assembled his five FNGs before the wire they had strung yesterday afternoon. He had them sit on the ground before him and paced calmly as he pointed at the barefoot Vietnamese man squatting on the other side of the rows of stacked and coiled razor-barbed wire. The small Vietnamese wore only a pair of rotting Jockey shorts. He stared through the wire with no emotion at all. His body was streaked with shining black camouflage grease; as black and shiny as his hair and eyes.

"Okay, listen up. You people," announced Frantz, "you will *not* die on me in combat. You FNGs will do everything to prove me wrong. You'll walk on trails, kick cans, sleep on guard, smoke dope, and diddily bop through the bush like you were back on the block." He narrowed his gaze at cocky Languilli. "When you're on guard at night, you will write letters, play with your organ, and think of your girl back home. *Forget* her. Some hairhead has her on her back right now and is telling her to fuck for peace."

The staff sergeant stopped pacing and pointed to the motionless Vietnamese before continuing the speech. "This is Han," he announced. "Those of you who are foolish will think of him as a gook, slope, slant, or dink. He is your enemy. He came over on the chieu hoi program. He will go back out there after he fattens up on C-rations and he *will* be hunting your young asses in the Ashau Valley."

On cue, Han picked up a B-40 rocket launcher, a pair of wire cutters, and a handful of rubber bands lying beside him. He slung the rocket launcher over his back and dropped his body first to all fours and then prone. He entered the wire like a snake, rolling and twisting silently, slowly and effortlessly, as he removed the smallest section of wire possible to allow him to move forward.

"Forget about Viet Cong shit," continued Frantz as the new troops stared bug-eyed at Han. Han placed rubber bands around the trip flares that had been so carefully embedded in the wire, to prevent them from going off as he spread the cut coils apart.

"What you will encounter out there," said Frantz, "are hard-core NVA, North Vietnamese Army troops. Motivated, highly trained, and well equipped. If you meet Han or his cousins, you will give him respect and refer to the little bastards as Nathaniel Victor. Meet him twice and survive, and you'll call him *Mr.* Nathaniel Victor." He again pointed to Han, who was moving effortlessly through the wire.

"People"—he squinted down at the FNGs—"I'm tired of filling body bags with your dumb fucking mistakes." The good-looking smart-ass Languilli was smiling.

"Do you think this is funny?" thundered Frantz. He looked at the FNG's name tag. "Alphabet," he called him.

The FNG's smile faded to a blushing frown. "Languilli," he told the N.C.O.

Deliberately ignoring him, Frantz glanced at Beletsky, who had looked away. "Han is crawling up on your position," he told him. "Look at me. I'm going to save your life and you're going to save mine. It's night. Raining. While you are thinking about Peace and Love and whether or not we should be in Vietnam, Han is going to cut your fucking throat." He then shot his eyes to Galvan, the stern-faced Chicano. "And you're sleeping."

"No, Sergeant," said Galvan calmly.

"You've been humping the boonies for months," countered Frantz. "You're tired. It's your turn to sleep. You're *allowed* to sleep. What do you think Han is going to do? Is he going to wake up Alphabet and smile and talk about women? *Mr.* Nathaniel Victor gets his rocks off watching you die! Some of you think you have problems because you are against the war, you demonstrated at school, you wear peace symbols on your steel pot, and you have *attitude* problems.'' He looked at each man in turn. "I'm an orphan. My brother's queer. The city of Chicago got the clap from my sister. Mom drinks. The old man coughs blood. I have ringworm, immersion foot, the incurable crud. And the draft ruined my chances of being a brain surgeon.'' He put his hands on his hips, without realizing it was the same gesture Worcester would have used. "People,'' he admonished, "you have no problem except me and *him.*''

Han, the former North Vietnamese Army regular, had now crawled all the way through the wire. Three feet from Frantz's side, he pushed himself to a crouch and pointed the tip of his rocket-propelled grenade at the FNGs. His face showed the same somber determination as Terry Frantz's.

Chapter Five

After shocking his new men with the demonstration of Han's slithering abilities, Terry Frantz let them join the rest of the squad for lunch and a swim at the authorized water point, near the bridge. He took them down the trail himself, but then immediately broke away from them.

The FNGs stood back, taking in the bizarre contrast of women leisurely hanging clothes to dry on a thin strand of barbed wire run beneath the bridge while children—perhaps cousins or even brothers and sisters of the sinister Han—played with the GIs. Terry Frantz was already naked and in the water by the time they reached the cluster of bushes where one troop who had already bathed stood guard over the others' clothes and weapons.

Frantz did not want to see the new boys' faces again. When they finally started into the water, he began swimming toward shore. He didn't want to cross their path again until it was absolutely necessary.

After drying and putting on the same stinking mud-streaked clothes, stockings, and boots, the N.C.O. pulled together the different C-ration meals that Doc, Motown, McDaniel, and Murphy had brought down with them. He then removed the cloth camouflage cover and plastic helmet liner from his steel pot. After rinsing the heavy steel pot in the river, he dumped all of the different meals in it, to make a C-ration stew. The recipe today was two cans greasy spaghetti, one can thin spiced and shredded beef, one can globular ham and lima beans, and one can even greasier beans and franks. As he stirred the concoction as best he could with a tiny white plastic spoon, another civilian transistor radio blared the latest from Armed Forces Radio in Saigon.

"The provost marshal has asked me to remind all military personnel that the Military Police will be giving DRs to any troops who have not rolled down their sleeves after six, in accordance with the anti-malaria program."

Frantz noticed that two of the FNGs had finally mustered the balls to challenge the old-timers to a water fight. Motown was on McDaniel's shoulders and Gaigin on Duffy's. Bienstock was atop Beletsky. The outnumbered recruits approached the splashing veterans timidly as the AFVN report moved on to the evening's base camp television schedule.

"Ed Sullivan, the Rogues, Bonanza, and College Bowl are featured on your AFVN television station tonight."

The jousting lasted only seconds, with Bienstock toppling, dragging Beletsky under with him. The two FNGs both kept losing their balance as Bienstock struggled to remount.

"In a major speech, the President has called upon the nation to turn back to religion to overcome what he called a crisis of spirit in America's youth."

Farther up the bank, Washburn stood comforting a whimpering little girl as Doc cleaned an infected sore on her arm. Three women and their children stood in line behind the little girl for the black man's services.

"Now here's a number-one favorite from the 'Young Rascals.' We'll dedicate it to the Redlegs with the Tropic Lightning at Cu Chi."

The music seemed to spur on the six water fighters, who merged for close-quarter combat and were all quickly toppled and dunked. They splashed and waved toward Frantz, who only smiled peacefully in response.

Glancing inadvertently up to the bridge, Frantz saw a trailer truck rumbling across. Instead of the normal olive drab flatbed trailer for hauling ammunition and supplies, this truck was pulling a gleaming blue-and-silver house trailer. It stopped at the end of the bridge, where Languilli and Galvan stood smoking and talking at the edge of the cyclone fence barrier strung before one of the APCs. The driver reached out of the cab and gave the full arm-in-fist "fuck you" gesture to the APCs he had just passed at the opposite end of the bridge.

"Hey, pal," he beseeched Languilli, "do you know where I can find a General Rufferman?"

"He's no friend of mine." Though still a cherry FNG, Languilli stared at the smooth-skinned driver with the disdain all grunts shared for rear echelon troops. The guy was a base camp commando, an REMF—rear-echelon motherfucker—who probably had never fired a weapon, never heard an incoming mortar round or rocket, and never seen spilled blood during his entire tour of duty. Unlike the grunts who had seen true shit, he would probably also go back to the World and tell war stories. Languilli hated him instantly.

"Major general," said the driver. "Two stars. I'm supposed to deliver this trailer to him."

"Did you try Phu Bai?" asked Galvan, with the same sarcasm as Languilli.

"I've been to Phu Bai, Danang, Hue, all the way up to Evans," lamented the frustrated driver. "I'm supposed to go *home* in nine days and I signed out for this damn thing and I can't find anybody to sign for it."

"I'll sign for it," said Languilli flatly.

The driver shook his head in frustration, not catching the humor. "I'm *responsible* for this. They'll keep me in the army forever to pay for it. Look at this." He leaned farther out the door and pointed back to the bullet holes that had peppered the trailer. "*Everybody* shoots at me. Especially you grunts! It's not *my* fault I spent a year at Qui Nhon with clubs and air-conditioned hooches and all that good stuff."

"That's hard-core," Galvan agreed, still not showing any emotion. Galvan, who took soldiering seriously and took pride in it, despised the base camp commando even more than Languilli did. Unlike Languilli, however, he didn't show it. His face remained as hard and cold as concrete.

"I'm like a rolling highway sign during hunting season," said the driver.

"Maybe you can find a marine to sign for it," suggested Galvan.

"Yeah. Thanks a lot, pal. Those guys *are* dense." The driver stuck his head back in and drove on through the village with no further comment or gesture. Languilli and Galvan stood watching the dust cloud rising behind it.

"This is one weird place," observed Galvan.

Languilli nodded in silent agreement.

Terry Frantz had been joined at his tiny makeshift C-ration kitchen by the four men whose meals he had mixed with his own, and did not notice the truck leave. Doc was now ladling Frantz's concoction into the empty C-ration cans that would serve as each man's bowl and plate. McDaniel and Motown were rubbing their hands in anticipation while the two whites—Murphy, the RTO, and Frantz, the cook-of-the-hour—lay back with their hands folded behind their heads and the sun piercing into their closed eyelids. The harsh sun felt refreshing rather than painful. When Frantz's can was ready, McDaniel leaned over to him and slapped his knee.

"I'm telling you. Seventeen and a wake-up and I don't ever have to eat this shit again. You know what I'm saying, Sarge?"

"You found a home in the army, Mac," said Frantz as he rose. "How are you going to act back in the World?" He noticed his five FNGs sitting in the dirt rather than squatting like the veterans. They were ten feet away, within earshot of the conversation. None of them had taken the trouble to make a stove and light a heat tab, not even Galvan. They were eating their individual meals from the original cans and were not talking.

"I got places to go, things to do, and people to see," said McDaniel.

Motown winked at Doc and Frantz as he egged his best friend on. "But how are you going to act?" he asked him, in his mellowest voice.

"Like a Pfc.," proclaimed McDaniel. "Private Fucking Civilian."

Motown shook his head and pointed as he kept teasing the innocent fellow-blood. "You are talking and you don't know what you are saying, brother," he told him. "You think you're ready for civilian life? Have you ever heard a boonie rat back in the World? How he talks? 'Fuck this, shit on that, no fucking way, I love that mother-fucking bastard, and why the fuck not?' ''

McDaniel hesitated before defending himself. He knew Motown was only teasing, but as short as he was, even the most lighthearted insinuation that life back in the States would be less than paradise struck a raw nerve. He was *ready* for the World. He would stop talking and acting like an animal the minute he boarded that gleaming jet, the freedom bird. "Back off, Motown. I've got my fucking act together . . ." He choked as he stopped to correct himself. "My act *is* together. My shit is straight."

After laughing at McDaniel's slip, Motown addressed the entire circle of stew eaters. "Do you know a straighter, more intelligent brother in First Platoon than me?" he asked.

No one answered but Doc stretched his neck and called over to the eavesdropping FNGs. "Listen up," he told them, "he's got college."

"One time," declared Motown proudly. He pivoted on his heels to address the newcomers. "When I went home on emergency leave, my mama made a special meal for me." His tone was still mellow but suddenly plaintive and melancholy. Everyone was listening intently. "She made everything that I love. Greens, fresh vegetables, potatoes, and I happen to love baked ham. My whole family is there and I say to myself, 'Motown, you have these people fooled.' The day before we were humping the Ashau Valley and now I'm home, with my family, and I'm skating." He spat at the side of the C-ration stove. The saliva sizzled and popped before evaporating. "No problem," he continued. "Number one. I smile at my mama: 'Great meal, Ma. Will you *please* pass the fucking potatoes? The ham's fucking A, Ma. You don't know how fucking great it is to be home.' " He turned abruptly to McDaniel. "How you gonna act?" he demanded to know, with no effort at hiding his bitterness.

McDaniel tried to act as if Motown had never said anything, as if the speech had had no effect. "Do you really want to know, Motown? I'm going to walk down Central Avenue in my jump boots and my medals," he declared. "It's going to be all right." He struggled to keep the tears back as he gazed into his friend's hopeless eyes.

"You better not wear your uniform," chimed in Beletsky from the FNG huddle. For Beletsky and the other new arrivals, the memories and images of what it *really* meant to be a GI in the civilian stateside world were still fresh and vivid. Beletsky had been forced to silently endure the draft-dodging college boys' remarks about his skinhead haircut as he entered the airport terminal for that long one-way flight. He had been forced to say nothing as the boys' girl friends called him a fucking baby-killer.

Lost for the moment in those indelible images, Beletsky jumped back and spilled his grape Kool-aid when the black medic leaped to his feet from the other group.

"Who's talking to you?" demanded Doc. The veins of his neck stood out like steel cords and his bulging eyes pierced right through the white boy. "This man has been fighting for the fucking United States of White America and you're trying to advise him that he can't wear his jump boots? New guys don't know *shit.*"

Blushing under both the black man's crazed stare and his own memories, Beletsky let it drop. Meekly. The guy would find out soon enough how the World really treated guys in jump boots. And he certainly didn't want Doc jumping any deeper in his own shit. Doc was in tight with everybody who mattered in the squad and Beletsky himself was still an outsider. Beletsky felt more pity for Doc than he did anger.

After lunch it was Languilli and Galvan's turn to go down to the water point. As they gathered their towels and plastic boxes of soap, the rest of the squad lounged around their bunkers. This was the normal routine when not on patrol: pull details like restringing wire, reinforcing the bunkers, and policing up the area in the morning; then lounge all afternoon waiting for the supply helicopter that would bring more ammunition, C-rations, and the most valued item of all, mail. The boredom of the daily routine, combined with the near-sleepless nights and the ever-present anticipation of the next patrol or rocket or sapper attack, made it impossible to truly relax even when there was nothing else to do.

Duffy and Gaigin, the machine-gun team; Murphy, the RTO; and McDaniel, the short-time blood, had spread a quilted green and brown camouflage-colored pancho liner atop their bunker and were playing hearts with a faded and worn deck of cards. Beletsky, after failing to get the message through to Doc and McDaniel about how they treated grunts back in the World, sat on the ground alone, writing to his beloved Claire.

Claire wasn't like the other college students. She would be proud of him, he told himself.

Motown was also off alone, cleaning his weapon, the same M16 that had jammed on him just a week ago; the same damned rifle that had caused him to chip a tooth biting into his towel.

Terry Frantz was also off to himself. He sat on the edge of a bunker with his steel pot and rifle at his side. He had pulled a letter from his helmet liner. After unfolding it with a surgeon's care, he was rereading it for the third time when Languilli and Galvan strolled past on their way to the path that led to the river.

Languilli was mimicking the lecture Doc had given on proper tooth-brushing form the previous evening. To his surprise, Galvan seemed to be reacting sympathetically to the kidding, actually smiling.

"You FNGs will listen to people who know. The commanding general believes that one of the most pressing problems we face in Vietnam is that of venereal disease," said Languilli, with a drill instructor's serious tone. "We have found that the best way to avoid contracting one of the nine known strands of syphilis and gonnorhea is by avoiding contact with the indigenous Vietnamese female personnel." Pulling a foil-wrapped condom from his breast pocket, he elbowed the Chicano in the ribs. "*However,*" he added, with a wink.

Galvan shook his head with a smile but kept his eyes on the trail ahead, even though they were in a completely secured area.

"Remember: *'Lai de homo kai,'*" Languilli continued. "*'Beaucoup dao tiem.'*"

"*'Lai de homo kai,'*" repeated Galvan. "*'Beaucoup dao tiem.'*"

"It means 'Come here and give me a kiss,'" explained Languilli. "'I love you too much.' It's the same anywhere, Galvan. You have to know the right words to score."

Ahead of them at the edge of the river, a little girl was washing her hair. She was about ten or eleven but from the tone of laughter coming from the bushes ahead at the end of the trail, Languilli knew she had older sisters and cousins nearby.

"I'm going back to get us some shampoo," said Languilli as he watched the little girl dig her fingers furiously into the thick white lather.

"Say again?" asked Galvan.

"It was in my Red Cross bag. We have to smell good for '*Lai de homo kai*.'"

Languilli had already turned around to go back up the trail as Galvan began to slowly repeat the phrase to himself: "*Lai de homo kai*." He smiled and kept repeating it as he continued toward the river.

Back at the bunker, Gaigin was watching Duffy. Taking a photo, he said, "Duffy, what are you doing?"

"It's called meditating, Gaigs."

"How do you know whether or not you're doing it right?"

"You feel your body start to float—"

Frantz leaped over the bunker shouting, "Incoming!"

Languilli trotted quickly but then stopped abruptly as he saw Duffy, Gaigin, Murphy, and McDaniel all diving from their bunker to the ground. At first he thought they might be chasing a snake or getting ready to run to the helicopter pad for mail.

"Incoming!" yelled Terry Frantz, lying prone at the side of the bunker.

"Hit it!" called Motown.

"Incoming!" repeated Frantz, but Languilli remained frozen and paralyzed. There were no explosions or small-arms fire in earshot. Yet.

"What's going on?" shrugged the FNG. "What—" Languilli finally cut himself off and dove into the foliage beside the steep trail as the first rounds finally arrived and exploded.

They kept coming steadily, in clusters of three. The explosions were not as loud or large as they would have been in a World War II movie. There was a small ball of fire at the center and the dirt clods and sandbags kicked up by the concussion looked almost harmless as they flew.

The true power of the tail-finned mortar rounds, however, was not visible to even the most careful eye. Their true power was their shrapnel, rather than the explosion. The metal itself was designed to sheer away in thin razor-sharp fragments. Bamboo stalks and tree limbs were easily severed by the invisible whizzing. The shrapnel was even capable of penetrating the GIs' steel pots.

Random voices were still screaming from the bunkers, "Incoming, incoming!"

The rounds kept hitting in clusters of three. There was a pause between each cluster as the enemy mortarmen reset their tubes to zero in on the bunkers.

The seasoned American veterans could make out the distant *thup, thup* noise of fresh rounds dropping into the tubes, hitting the firing pin at the bottom, and being sent on their way in a high arch. The veterans all again repeated the ominous cry "Incoming" each time they waited for the whistling and impact. They yelled as much for the psychological diversion of yelling *something* as to warn the FNGs.

Terry Frantz saw a PRC-25 lying atop a bunker and ran for it between clustered explosions. Curled beside the bunker, he reached up and grabbed the black plastic handset at the same time he pulled a plastic-laminated map from his wide flappy leg pocket.

"Cold Steel!" he cried into the handset. "Check-point Five Two, over." He released the *push-to-talk* button and awaited the reply. The voice at the other end came in crackling with static and barely audible. "Five Two, this is Cold Steel, over."

"Fire mission!" yelled Frantz. "Over," he added calmly.

"Say again," replied the radio.

"Fire mission from Violet Three Alpha, right One Zero Zero H.E. Fire for effect."

Beyond Frantz's corner of the bunker, a voice he couldn't recognize was yelling across the perimeter.

"Medic!" the voice cried. "Doc! Doc, over here!"

The enemy mortar rounds continued coming in neat groups of three. That meant, at least, that there were just three tubes and that it was just an after-noon exercise in harassment rather than a prelude to a serious ground attack. If the enemy were serious, he would have encircled the village and sent in just one quick stunning barrage with at least three times that many tubes before storming the wire. Such se-rious attacks, Terry Frantz and all the other veterans knew, were nearly always held back until the cover of night.

As Frantz continued struggling to communicate with the artillery battery that was two mountain ridges away, Doc responded quickly to the anony-mous cry for help. He ran in a crouch, rifle dan-gling in one hand as the other hand clasped the flopping steel helmet to his head. The canvas med-ical bag, slung over his shoulder, flapped wildly against his hip. He grit his teeth and ran a little faster each time he heard the soft *thup* of the unseen tubes. The cry was coming from near the trail that led to the water point. Doc ran into the bush rather than chance the open trail.

Motown, meanwhile, had dived next to Frantz and the radio. He checked his M16's chamber quickly but thoroughly before slapping closed the barrel, trigger assembly, and stock. Frantz nudged him and pointed to the tree line at the far edge of the rice field, between attempts to raise their Redleg brethren on the radio.

"They're correcting on us," panted Frantz to the rifleman. "They must have a spotter in that tree line."

"Roger that." Motown nodded. As soon as Motown opened up on the tree line, with his rifle on rock-and-roll and working smoothly, he was joined by Duffy and Gaigin and their trusty pig at the next bunker.

The artillery battery finally gave Frantz the high-sign during the firing.

"Stand by for rounds," warned the calm crackling voice.

"Standing by!" yelled Frantz.

"Rounds out."

"Rounds out," echoed Frantz before joining Motown and spraying the dense green with his own rifle. By now, everyone in the perimeter had realized that the mortar rounds were being adjusted by a spotter hiding with a radio somewhere in the bush. Everyone was spraying methodically yet randomly, with no idea exactly where the man might be.

By the time the first friendly artillery rounds began landing in the area where Frantz had guessed the mortar tubes might be placed, the enemy exercise had already been completed. The spotter was either dead or long gone—probably long gone—and the mortar crews were probably scampering through the bush with no fear of the artillery hitting them.

Frantz called out to the troops to cease fire as the friendly artillery barrage commenced. In such triple canopy jungle, even the GIs knew the odds were at least twenty-to-one against actually hitting the unseen enemy. The artillery barrage was ultimately more a psychological reaction than a concerted attempt to nail any particular individual, and both sides knew it. It was part of the ritual of any ambush, as were air strikes if it were convenient. The stalking enemy was nearly always long gone before any of the Americans' high technology firepower began the ritual of raping and razing the bamboo and teakwood rain forest.

Doc stood calmly by the edge of the trail, near the river, as everyone above regrouped. Frantz and Motown, who had seen him dash into the bush, trotted down to his side.

A pair of legs and boots extended from the edge of the foliage into the trail at Doc's feet but none of the rest of the body was visible.

"Who is it?" asked Frantz.

"I don't know," Doc said with a shrug, staring at the new boots. "He's got no goddam head. It's one of the new guys." He looked earnestly into Frantz's eyes. "You *have* to tell these men to put an extra set of ID tags on their boots, man. One each. *Then* this shit wouldn't happen."

"It's not Wishbone," said Motown, meaning to say Washburn. "That dude is white."

"How am I supposed to identify these people?" implored Doc, trembling.

"Take it easy, Doc," said Frantz, stepping closer but afraid to touch him.

"I'll take it any way I can." Doc stared defiantly at the small blood-filled crater above the body's tattered shoulders and outstretched arms. "I *have* to know who you are. I'm supposed to know."

Doc did not notice Bienstock walk past him. The New Yorker glanced inquisitively toward the body but then immediately jerked his head up toward the bunkers. He saw Beletsky standing awkwardly beside a bunker and ran to him quickly. Beletsky was a pain with his never-ending questions and worrying, but now his familiar face was a welcome sanctuary.

Another man soon emerged from the bush beside the trail. His face and chest were covered with thick mud. Frantz picked up the olive drab towel that had been dropped in the trail, probably by the dead man, and threw it at him. As the mud came off the face, everyone immediately recognized Languilli, Alphabet.

Doc was now squatting next to the body, with a copper-wired brown tag in his hand. Terry Frantz was finally nauseous as he knelt at Doc's side.

"Galvan," the squad leader said to the new boots. "His name is Galvan."

Doc showed no reaction as he accepted the pencil Frantz pulled from his thigh pocket.

"Galvan," Frantz repeated, "Private First Class."

Doc still showed no sign of recognition or interest as he filled in the brown form.

As usual, the best of the bunch had been the one to buy the farm. Terry Frantz regretted having even bothered to size up the five FNGs. He was sorry he had spotted Galvan as the one with the makings of a solid soldier that first morning, when the Chicano had pulled the tape from his pocket and attached a second magazine to his rifle in imitation of his squad leader.

Chapter Six

The next day, with Bravo Company still awaiting orders for its next patrol or combat assault, the company commander authorized 3rd Squad three hours at the whorehouse just beyond the company's sector of the village defense perimeter. He knew the rumors were all over that they would be going back into the dreaded Ashau Valley, Vietnam's equivalent of what no-man's-land had been in World War I (where possession shifted from one side to the other on a continuing basis and where a few meters of ground fought over desperately could be abandoned by Higher before all the wounded and dead were even extracted). The Ashau Valley's triple canopy jungle, free of villages but streaked with supply trails coming in from across the border of Laos and Cambodia, was the turf of the NVA rather than the Viet Cong guerrillas. It was one of the few places in Vietnam where the Americans were likely to fight the equivalent of a conventional battle, against a fully equipped battalion or division.

The company commander knew only too well that 3rd Squad, 1st Platoon, had been decimated in the Ashau recently and that they had now lost one of their FNG replacements to the fluke of a mortar round launched in broad daylight. He knew they had to have a break in the tension if he wanted them at their peak for tomorrow's still-secret helicopter combat assault. He would let the platoon leader know about the CA that evening, after they were primed with the girls and beer. After Mama-san's, they would be confident and cocky, ready to kick ass and take no names.

Frantz and Worcester were the last ones to leave the company area. They strolled leisurely along the red dirt road, unlike the others (even the veterans) who ran toward the waiting whorehouse with the unbridled excitement of grade school children. When the two staff sergeants finally arrived, Mama-san herself was waiting for them in the well-maintained house's doorway.

Unlike most of the rest of the village's thatch-roofed houses, Mama-san's place was freshly painted. It even had the remnants of a grass lawn and a neatly kept walkway up to the low wooden porch, not unlike an American house. The only signs of Vietnam were the fighting bunker just ten feet beside it and the typical thatch roof.

"Sergeant Worcester," Mama-san called, waving, "where you been so long?" Her near-toothless grin seemed to cover her entire shriveled face. She nodded enthusiastically as she spoke. Like all her girls, she wore an American-style dress rather than the Vietnamese *au-dai.*

Mama-san had reserved two of her best girls for the NCOs. She led the men directly to the steam room, not even pausing to let them order a beer in the larger room of small Formica tables and kitchen-style metal-legged chairs where the other Americans were already whooping it up.

Frantz and Worcester were both grateful that none of the other troops noticed their entrance. Anticipat-

ing what was waiting beyond the plastic curtain that
led to the massage tables and then the solid American-style door that led to the steaming large square
tub, Terry Frantz already had a hard-on.

Debbie and Kathy were waiting with cold bottles
of Bami-bam beer in their hands and white towels
wrapped around their bodies. The towels were
tucked just above their nipples and barely covered
their thin pubic hair. Both girls' delicate shoulders
glowed in the dim light. Despite the Western names
Mama-san had given them (and despite the Western
manners they had picked up from their trade), their
smiles and giggling were still refreshingly innocent
to Terry Frantz's eyes and ears.

"This water is beaucoup hot, girl-san," said
Worcester, testing the steaming water with a finger
after the first long chug of beer. "Number ten."

"I like it hot," said Frantz as Kathy began help-
ing unbutton the mud-stiffened fatigue jacket. "I
want to get this red dirt *out* of my body."

"You can take a hundred baths and you'll still
sweat the 'Nam," said Worcester.

"You two not MPs, are you?" asked Kathy as
she watched both men step gingerly into the tub.
Their necks and forearms were almost as tan as her
own flesh but the rest of their lean hard bodies was
deathly pale. She tried not to giggle at the youngest
one's anxious erection and the thick black hair behind it. Like all Vietnamese, she was repulsed by
the hair and smell of the Americans' bodies. Like
all her countrymen, she was also offended but helpless to respond when the Americans referred to Vietnamese girls as "titless and hairless snatch."

Kathy's co-worker Debbie was already leaning
over the tub to wash the older troop's back. "MP's
number ten thousand, man," she said as she set his

beer on the edge of the tub and picked up a thick sponge. "They boom-boom all the time and never pay. Me and Kathy love grunts."

"We're first-class mud rollers," said Worcester as he sank up to his chin.

"Number-one massage I give," said Debbie, reaching her hand in the water and leaning closer with her sweetly perfumed torso. "You like so much you take me back to the World with you."

"To the big PX," said Worcester.

"Fucking A," said Debbie, the way a GI would have, with no thought of the obscenity of the word.

"Don't you love Vietnam?" asked Frantz as he set down his empty bottle and joined his friend in the water.

"Vietnam number one," said Kathy as she took up her position, kneeling behind him and placing her thin fingers on his shoulders.

"Number ten after we *didi-mau*," said Frantz. "VC don't have any money for boom-boom."

"And they got little dicks," added Worcester, guiding Debbie's hand under the water.

"Same-same Marvin the ARVN," said Frantz, closing his eyes and doing the same with Kathy's hand.

"ARVN is useless," agreed Debbie, rising higher on her knees to get closer to her work. "He's tired of fighting your fucking war," she added as she removed the towel with the other hand, letting it fall at her side.

"*My* fucking war? My *fucking* war?" asked Worcester, with eyebrows drawn, not even noticing the girl's nipples as he twisted his neck to confront her.

"Come on. *Our* fucking war," concurred Frantz, winking at Kathy for her to mimic her friend's gesture. Kathy giggled as the towel fell away to reveal her erect brown nipples.

"I no bullshit you," Debbie told her client. "GI *like* to fight. Vietnamese just want to short-time and—"

"And PX privileges," interrupted Frantz, lifting his arms to help Kathy into the water.

"There it is," said Debbie as she too stepped into the large square tub.

"GIs never leave," said Kathy, floating before Frantz, with her hands straddling his thighs on the bottom of the porcelain. "No question."

"As you were, Worcester," said Frantz as he pulled her closer. "As you were." He then spoke directly to Kathy's sparkling black eyes. "The question is," he mused, "how many of us do you have to boom-boom before those mean little bastards from the North show up. That's the question."

Worcester showed his agreement and dropped the subject with a loud yell as he too pulled his giggling girl closer. He yelled again as he saw Frantz and Kathy sink completely beneath the steaming water.

After the steam room tryst, the two NCOs put on the same stinking muddy jungle fatigues and boots. Both girls put on the sleeveless blouses and tight miniskirts that were the uniform-of-the-day at Mamasan's place. The girls were fully clothed and holding their hands out for their payment before the GIs had their boots laced. There was no emotion on their faces as they waited for the wrinkled pink and blue military-script bills. They nodded thanks and turned to join the action in the main room without even kissing their pale lovers good-bye. Both men were past history and would remain so unless they came up with the script for another ten-minute session.

The rest of 3rd Squad was partying strong and wild, just as their commanding officer had wanted them to. When Worcester and Frantz finally appeared, Debbie was already dancing with the bloods Washburn and McDaniel. Kathy was sitting beside Bienstock in one of the chrome-legged dining chairs, stroking his leg as she watched her friend dance with the two huge black men. The red shower curtain that sectioned off one corner of the room for "short-time" action was closed, indicating that a couple were going at it.

Mama-san was scurrying among the tables to make sure no one ran dry of the bitter Bami-bam beer. She paused to wave to the two veteran customers and then pointed to a free table.

"I go *beaucoup dinky-dau* every time I see you, Mama-san," called Frantz.

"You have to come more often," she said. "The marines, they love this place."

Frantz noticed for the first time the different banners and unit insignias that adorned the room's Formica-paneled walls. In addition to the 101st Airborne Division's screaming eagle, there was the ivy leaf of the Famous Fighting 4th Infantry Division, based at Pleiku; the strawberry with a lightning bolt in the center from the 25th Infantry Division, Tropic Lightening, out of Cu Chi; the horse and black slash of the 1st Air Cavalry at An Khe; and the eagle, anchor, and globe of the U.S. Marine Corps.

It looked like everyone had been laid here. There were even a white-starred flag from the FLN, the National Liberation Front, which was the official organization of the various Viet Cong units all over the country, and the duller plain-numbered banners of a few individual NVA regiments. Frantz wasn't sure whether the enemy banners were gifts from the

GIs or marines or if the enemy too had gotten their rocks off at Mama-san's place.

"You can fart in a balloon, paint it red, and a marine would love it," said Worcester.

Mama-san now hovered over Bienstock's shoulder. "Why don't you go in back with Kathy?" she asked. "She almost never do it."

"The girl-san has *Skyhawks* tattooed across her snatch," called Terry Frantz, blushing as he watched Kathy work on the FNG's thigh.

Mama-san whirled and glowered at Frantz. "You probably too big for her," she said sarcastically.

Ignoring her, Frantz looked directly at Bienstock. "What's Alphabet doing?" he asked.

Bienstock shrugged. "I don't know."

Again annoyed at how the FNGs refused to think of their buddies, to think as a unit rather than individuals, Frantz unconsciously put his hands on his hips. "You *should*," he told him.

"He's eating her!" laughed Doc, from the next table.

"You white dudes are *most* strange about that," chimed in Motown, strolling by with a beer in each hand and then stopping at Doc's table. The two bloods dapped as the curtains opened and a somber Vincent Languilli emerged. Languilli's girl still lingered on the military cot, adjusting her blouse.

"Hey," Doc called to Bienstock, who was finally reciprocating Kathy's moves on her own thigh. "What are you doing in Vietnam, *boy?*"

Bienstock froze. The black medic's eyes glared at him savagely. Kathy's soft fingers were completely forgotten. "I volunteered," he managed to stammer to his interrogator.

"The *brothers* are here because they are black and undereducated," explained Doc, challenging him.

"That's bullshit," declared Languilli, still standing before the plastic shower curtain as the girl brushed passed him with her military script wadded in her hand.

Doc's legs shot the chair back as he rose to confront the new honky's challenge. The chair fell over backward behind him. "Say *what*, FNG?" he demanded, clenching his fists.

Languilli took just one step forward and slugged the black man squarely in the jaw, flooring him.

Motown was then on top of Languilli, sending him sprawling, before the white lover-boy's eyes had moved from Doc's flying boots.

Platoon Sergeant Worcester then flew atop Motown. Rather than take on the black rifleman, he went for Languilli, who was on the bottom. He rolled Languilli over in a tight headlock to break them apart.

"Slack off, Alphabet!" ordered Frantz, standing over the bodies with his feet spread and his hands on his hips in the calm drill instructor pose.

Languilli finally managed to break Worcester's grip, to everyone's amazement. Rather than counterattack, however, he only sat up and rubbed his throat.

Motown and Doc were both back on their feet. Motown was holding Doc back from the white boy with a bear hug.

"My name isn't 'Alphabet,' " the dazed FNG told his squad leader. "It's Languilli. *Vinnie*. My first name is Vinnie." Glancing at Bienstock and his emotionless Vietnamese whore, suddenly disgusted with what he had just done and with everyone and everything around him, he cleared his throat and again confronted the black medic. "*Vincent*," he told Doc. Still confronting the black man's eyes, he pointed down at the metal dog tag he had laced into his boot. "What's my name, Doc?"

The room was stone silent. Motown eased the pressure around Doc's chest but Doc did not lurch forward toward the man who had been his nemesis just seconds ago. With the boot gesture, everyone in the room now realized the bad bummer Languilli was going through. Languilli had been with the headless man at the trail going down to the water point. Doc himself now realized for the first time that this was the man who had emerged covered with mud while he himself had knelt cursing the dead body for not having ID tags in its boots.

"Your name is Vincent," said Doc soothingly.

Frantz motioned for Bienstock to take his buddy outside. Bienstock didn't even notice the pout on Kathy's face as he pushed her aside.

As Bienstock helped Languilli to his feet, Worcester and Doc each approached the shaking troop with a fresh beer. They gave the bottles to Bienstock, who followed his fellow-FNG through the door of the house out into the glaring sun.

"You GIs are all *beaucoup dinky-dau*," said Mama-san, standing by helplessly but thankful that no furniture had been broken.

"Ruck out, Mama-san!" commanded Frantz, glaring into the shriveled woman's eyes. She looked to be fifty years old but Frantz knew she was closer to thirty.

Mama-san chose the better part of valor and did not react to the foreign client's insolence. She had been around American soldiers plenty long enough to know when to shut up and when to fleece them. Now was the time to shut up. She would have them all fleeced by dusk, anyway.

Bienstock followed Languilli to the bunker adjacent to the house. They both looked off silently at the villagers working the rice fields. Women in wide bamboo hats were walking quickly atop the high narrow dikes, stooping only slightly under the long poles balanced across their shoulders. The circular hats glared in the sun and the heavy buckets of earth at each end of the poles bounced up and down.

Several children were loitering across the street from the whorehouse. They started to approach the two GIs for the customary C-ration cigarettes and candy but backed off as soon as they saw the faces clearly. Like Mama-san, they had learned long ago how to read the foreigners' open-book faces. They knew when to back off and when to move in for a score.

Languilli took a beer from Bienstock. "I'm back there looking at my first piece of ass since I got here," he explained to no one, trembling. "And all I can think about is 'What the hell was that guy's first name?' And it *wasn't* FNG!"

"Tony," volunteered Bienstock, handing him Doc's beer. "Or Billy, Frankie. Let me think: Johnnie, Bobbie, Billy . . ."

"I think it began with an *S,* or an *A,*" mused Languilli, his voice now calm.

"Eddie," suggested Bienstock.

Languilli took a long swig of the beer. "Bamibam tastes like panther piss," he observed.

"Abe," said Bienstock, himself now absorbed in the name game.

" 'Abe'?" Languilli stared incredulously at his buddy. "He was a *Chicano,* Bienstock!"

Bienstock could not believe Alphabet too was going to dig in his shit. "I'm trying to help you, Languilli," he reminded him. "It was *my* turn behind the curtain and here I am playing 'What's His Name' with you.'' He kicked the red dirt at Languilli's feet.

"I never thought Jewish guys got horny,'' said Languilli calmly, with deliberate cruelty.

"No. No. Not to me. Alphabet.''

The nickname finally broke Languilli out of his trance. Blushing, he suddenly realized what an asshole he had been. But he did not know how to apologize or back off without looking like an even bigger ass. He shrugged imploringly to Bienstock and said in a near-whisper, "I just got to know.''

"Antonio,'' interrupted Terry Frantz, standing five feet behind them, near Mama-san's doorway. "Antonio Galvan.''

Languilli knew his face was crimson but still could not force himself to release his true emotion. He could not let himself look like a pussy. "Antonio . . . It don't mean nothing,'' he said firmly, tossing the Bami-bam bottle into the dirt road and pivoting to lead Bienstock back into the whorehouse.

Chapter Seven

Terry Frantz and Douglas Worcester walked back toward the Bravo Company command post alone that evening, with the rest of 3rd Squad still partying strong inside Mama-san's neatly painted thatch-roof whorehouse. As they walked, neither man noticed the glorious sunset occurring on their left.

Ironically, evening in this area of operation, where both sides suffered constantly high casualties without gaining anything smacking of victory, was like a scene from a picture postcard. Now the distant mountain peaks were going through the final phase of a rainbow, moving from deep red to purple. The rice fields' symmetrical squares of water gleamed like delicate panes of stained glass between the straight mud dikes. The thatch-roofed houses all had lanterns inside, glowing soft and yellow through the glassless windows, and the air itself was cool and sweet with the mixed smells of incense and frying rice.

For Frantz and Worcester, however, the setting might as well have been the same dull corner they had walked by every day back in the old neighborhood. Their senses were numb to beauty and exotica.

Frantz's mind was still on Vincent Languilli's outburst and Antonio Galvan's untagged boots rather than the magnificent sunset, the playacting girls back at Mama-san's or even the imminent return to the grueling heat and foliage of the NVA-infested Ashau Valley. He had been through it all too many times. It was finally getting to him.

Worcester knew Frantz was brooding, and knew better than to try to snap him out of it. Everybody deserved to do a little brooding, now and then. They had earned the right.

Frantz himself finally broke the silence by quoting his own earlier vow to the FNGs. " 'People, you will not die on me in combat,' " he told Worcester, without turning from the road ahead to look at him. "The kid was *good*," he then declared, letting at least some of the frustration escape. "He did everything right. What difference does it make? We've been up and down this same terrain since I *got* here. For what?"

The cynical, self-pitying words finally pricked the nerve of Worcester's professionalism. He might let his friend get away with a few minutes' sulking, but never *that* kind of garbage. "When you get home," he said firmly, "you can throw away your boots, grow a beard, and become a goddam hippie protestor. But I don't want to *hear* that shit in First Platoon."

"I know too many names, Worcester." Frantz looked up to the moon and stars as if in search of a supportive listener. "Too many names." He then confronted the lifer squarely, eyeball to eyeball. "And I don't think one of them is worth all of *Vietnam, Republic of.*"

"Don't fall apart on your people, Frantz," commanded Worcester, without flinching.

"Why, so I can teach them how to fill sandbags, burn shit?"

"They will need you back in the Ashau Valley. We're going back in." Worcester paused, waiting for a reaction, but there was none. He was tempted to floor him. "What the hell do you think I took you here for?" he demanded. "Your people are going to *die* unless you get your head out of your ass, Young Stuff."

Terry Frantz remained frozen in the red dirt as Worcester turned and marched away from him in disgust. Frantz suddenly noticed the laughter and yells coming from Mama-san's place; suddenly felt a chill in the windless twilight as he noticed the last magnificent sliver of sun falling rapidly beyond the deep distant peaks of the Ashau Valley.

Worcester had been right. Damn him.

Get your head *out* of your ass, Frantz told himself as he trotted to catch up with him.

By the time the sun returned to the still rice paddies next morning, in a soft radiant yellow, every man in Bravo Company's sector of the village defense perimeter was going through his own private ritual to psyche himself up for the combat assault into the Ashau Valley.

Officers and NCOs in full fighting gear were studying checkpoints on maps and checking their watches every few seconds, even though the checkpoints had been thoroughly memorized and the precise time of arrival was irrelevant at this point in the game.

A chaplain flown in from base camp the previous day was offering communion to the Catholics and anyone else—lapsed Catholics, atheists, Jews—who wanted the comfort of a gesture of trust and hope in

God. As was always the case before a combat assault, his ratio of takers was about two dozen times higher than back at Camp Evans.

Combat assault: CA: Charlie Alpha. The term didn't stir any more emotion or curiosity from the watchers of the six o'clock news back in the World than did any of the other interesting jargon—*hot LZ, dust off, search and destroy, greeneye, KIA, arc light mission.* All of the cryptic terms were in one way or another shorthand for protracted misery and/ or quick death. CA, however, was the one cryptic mission that made all the others seem routine by comparison—at least in the grunts' minds.

CA meant insertion into unknown terrain by helicopter. It meant flying in the doorless cargo bay with your knees jammed into your chest or your legs dangling above the skid, unable to hear anything going on between the pilot and Higher or anything happening on the ground below; unable to even see the ground for the deceptively soft green canopy of teakwood forest that could easily hide a bunker complex or even an artillery battery; unable to do anything except pray and scan for muzzle flashes as the bird approached the target landing zone and you prepared to jump.

The four remaining FNGs of 3rd Squad still did not appreciate what the two simple words *combat assault* implied, but they knew from the nervous flurry of activity around them and the sharpness of everyone's voice that it was not going to be the same as a ride in a deuce-and-a-half truck. They stood awkwardly above their packed and bulging rucksacks and their cleaned rifles, not knowing what to do with their hands and again feeling isolated from everyone else.

Doc was checking his medical supplies and repacking them neatly and tightly into his canvas shoulder-slung bag.

Duffy and Gaigin were trying to get in one more full hand of hearts with their faded playing cards while others readjusted their ruck straps to minimize the biting and cutting into the shoulders.

The FNGs kept darting from one routine to another. They tried to ignore the quiet determination on Staff Sergeant Frantz's face as he first tapped a magazine against his steel pot to make sure it was clean and then taped it upside down to the magazine already in his rifle.

They tried to hide their puzzlement as Motown pulled a can of peaches from a pile of discarded but unopened C-rations and stuck it into a stretched green sock to tie to his rucksack frame.

"I bet we're the lead bird again," Motown called to Frantz as he finished tying the sock.

Beletsky turned to the black man with unabashed fear in his eyes. "That's good, isn't it?" he asked.

Motown only shrugged, giving no answer. "It is if they want to let us land and get the dudes behind us," he reassured Worrier. He then frowned, however, adding, "Or they might just ding us and *di-di mau.*"

"So it's not good," concluded Beletsky. He then turned to Bienstock. "What do you think?" he asked.

Bienstock only closed his eyes and slowly shook his head back and forth. Bienstock appeared to be more worried than Beletsky, this time. The steel pot looked large enough to hold two heads the size of his. There was a delay each time it moved as he kept shaking his head.

It reminded Beletsky of a turtle lost in its own shell. Bienstock was sitting on his rucksack with his M16 propped upright between his legs, unconsciously tapping the barrel against the moving helmet.

Vincent Languilli was also sitting atop his rucksack, with his legs spread apart, scratching the inside of his left thigh. "I think I got the creeping crud," he told the trembling Beletsky, trying to divert his thoughts from today's mission, whatever it might be.

Murphy, standing behind Languilli and hunching his shoulders forward to balance himself under the weight of his PRC-25 and the rest of the gear and food in his pack, laughed wildly at the FNG's apparent naïveté.

"*I* busted her cherry," he boasted, tapping the black plastic radio handset. He had wrapped the handset in a discarded clear plastic bag to protect it from the rain and chest-deep streams he knew they would soon confront.

"You might have made a dent," countered Washburn, the soft-spoken Georgian.

" 'I love you too much,' she says," lamented Languilli as he kept scratching. " 'You owe it to yourself,' I says."

Languilli did not notice the veterans turn their faces away from his performance. The other FNGs, even Beletsky, were still watching him. They only kept watching him, however, because their ears were not yet tuned to detect the barely discernible but already increasing *whup-whup* noise of distant rotary blades.

"Ruck up," commanded Terry Frantz, slipping into the shoulder straps of his own rucksack and rising in one smooth motion. He motioned for 3rd

Squad to gather around him in a circle, to be ready
to run down to the sandbag landing pad and board
their bird as soon as the signal came.

The six helicopters came in like flitting mosquitoes, in single file, with their rotors invisible but
slapping loud. They flew over the village at high altitude and then banked steeply, causing the rotors'
slapping to intensify and catching a momentary glint
of sun on their dull snub noses. They came in one
at a time, with all the others continuing to circle as
each one split off in turn.

The pilots kept the noses pointed upward as they
approached the tiny pad, ready for a quick lift-off.
The men on the ground pressed their helmets to their
heads and leaned almost violently into the whirling
dirt and stones kicked up by the rotors.

Terry Frantz waited for that first bird to arch back
up toward the sun before finally briefing his men on
their mission. Beletsky showed neither relief nor apprehension upon realizing that they would not be the
lead bird.

"Now, people!" yelled Frantz, to the FNGs
rather than the rest of the squad. "We pay for our
mistakes out there! Alert, alive!" He glanced over
his shoulder at the second descending helicopter. It
actually looked hollow and fragile, with the huge
empty doorless cargo bay. "We are going into the
Ashau Valley!" he announced. "If you encounter
people not friendly toward you . . . *kill* them!"

With the second bird lifting off, the shirtless man
who was serving as traffic guide at the pad finally
waved to Frantz. Frantz motioned silently for his
men to move out and led them quickly down to the
pad.

The FNGs right behind him smiled as they caught
brief snatches of other N.C.O.s and officers still

trying to get their troops organized. The FNGs were
for the first time reassured that they weren't the only
people in Vietnam who still didn't have their act together.

"Move out . . . "

"Line up . . . "

"*Wake* up, troop . . . "

"Stay away from the rear rotary blades . . . "

"Radioman, put that antenna down . . . "

"Move out, you scroungy-assed bastards . . . "

When they reached the pad, Frantz motioned for
them to stay back and then took his position at the
edge of the square of sandbags. He motioned the
barebacked traffic controller aside and proceeded to
guide the bird in himself. Holding his rifle above his
head horizontally with both hands, he squinted directly into the backwash and the snub nose and the
faceless dark-visored pilot.

From the pilot's perspective, Frantz and all the
rest of 3rd Squad looked like bloated dying insects
as they crouched under their gear. Each rucksack
weighed more than eighty pounds with its combi-
nation of C-rations, ammunition, flares, foot powder, bayonet, extra socks, mosquito repellant, air
mattress, pancho liner, and collapsible entrenching
tool. Most men had tucked a green towel under their
collars, imitating the bloods, in a vain effort to ease
the cutting of the straps into their shoulders. They
squirmed as the full weight forced the jagged edge
of a foot powder can here and a bandolier of M16
rounds there into their ribs and kidneys.

Ducking and running to the side of the bird to get
his men inside, Frantz noticed the piece of plastic
over the muzzle of Languilli's rifle. There was no
time to compliment him, however.

Frantz knelt at the edge of the high, shiny, corrugated metal floor and extended a hand to each man as he leaped. First came Motown, then Duffy, Alphabet, Bienstock.

They all ignored the pain of the unheard jingling and flapping of bullets and other hard jagged objects against their bones. Each man followed the preceding one's footsteps precisely as he ran and charged toward the floor with his rifle held as far from him as possible and at shoulder level.

The veterans made it inside easily, in a single leap, landing on their feet in a squatting position and quickly moving farther in for the next man. Each of the FNGs, however, balked at the last step under the weight of the rucksack. Each FNG threw his chest against the metal and then made it the rest of the way in with Staff Sergeant Frantz pushing hard on his buttocks.

The new men's awkwardness didn't matter, however. Nor did the pain or the weight on their backs. They were all one unit, all being borne together into the same maelstrom.

They all smiled defiantly, with a few of them flashing the peace sign to the pad man, as the vibrating bird lifted off and arched quickly back in the direction of the distant bluish ridge.

They were 3rd Squad, 1st Platoon, Bravo Company, all of them. The rest of the world didn't give a shit for them and they cared even less for the rest of the world. *They* were going into the Ashau Valley. To hell with the rest of the world.

Chapter Eight

The six helicopters flew in a wide staggered formation, all the grunts pointing their rifle barrels downward to avoid shooting one of the intricate hoses in the turbine and rotary assembly should the weapons discharge accidentally or for whatever other reason. The door gunners peered intently down at the thick treetops, with their plastic flight helmets glaring and even their clean nylon flak jackets occasionally glinting. One of the gunners in 3rd Squad's bird wore a purple ascot and had painted the calling-card phrase *Death and Destruction, Call Day or Night* on the large canister that fed the endless belts of ammunition to his weapon. The gunner on the other side of the bird had written *Janice* on his flight helmet and *Doors* on his protective vest.

Troops in one bird would occasionally wave or flash the peace sign to those in the nearest ship. Some of them rolled down their shirt sleeves and turned up their collars against the coldness of the altitude and wind.

Terry Frantz, however, removed his steel pot and let the cold wind beat full force into his face and hair. He sat on the edge, next to the door gunner who was a Janis Joplin and Doors freak, with his feet dangling and the wind whipping his bloused trousers into balloons. He was wondering what must be going through the minds of his FNGs when the door gunner tapped his shoulder and pointed a thumb down toward the treetops, the signal that they were preparing to drop.

With the adrenaline pumping and with all his senses on full alert (including some senses he still didn't realize he had), Frantz slapped the steel pot back on his head. He scooted farther from the floor's edge; far enough out to touch the skid with his boot. When he tapped the man next to him to get ready and pass the signal along to the others, the door gunner was already laying down covering fire with his self-feeding M60 machine gun.

They were going in quicker than Frantz realized. Squinting into the tree line, he stood on the skid with one hand clasping the edge of the door gunner's seat and the other holding the M16 rifle's pistol-grip handle, ready to fire.

So far, so good; he could see no yellow flashes or red or green streaks to indicate small arms fire. The target landing zone was a small field of elephant grass at the base of a gentle and lightly wooded slope that quickly turned into a hill that was steep and high enough to be called a mountain in some parts of the world.

The squad leader jumped before the skid even touched the tips of the waving three-foot-tall, razor-sharp blades of grass, landing on his feet. Everyone else was out within twenty seconds and the bird was back on its way, whining and flitting and slanting its nose downward for more speed, without ever having touched down. Frantz waited in the grass to greet each man with a hand signal toward the tree line, where they were to regroup with the rest of 1st Platoon. Frantz took a head count without even knowing why, and was the last man into the bush.

No one had yet had time to even privately give thanks that it had been a cold LZ. Ahead of Frantz, Platoon Sergeant Worcester was pulling Lieutenant Eden by the strap of his rucksack. The two finally collapsed at the edge of the tree line beside what seemed to be a thicker and blacker blade of grass but was actually the antenna of Murphy's PRC-25.

Worcester grabbed the plastic-wrapped handset from his RTO with no comment, ignoring the panting green lieutenant at his feet. "Blackjack, Blackjack," he called, in a loud whisper. "This is Papa Bear, over."

"Blackjack, over," replied the calm radio voice.

"Papa Bear is down," Worcester reported. "Negative contact, LZ secure. Bring in the little bears, over." Relaxing his grip on the handset, he yelled to all the squad leaders who knelt around him awaiting their specific orders.

"Meyer, Frantz, Smitty, move your people *out!*" he yelled. As the other NCOs turned away to obey, he refocused on his hyperventilating new lieutenant. Thinking of all the other lieutenants he had broken in, of how they had all been as helpless and dazed as this one on their first hump but how they had transformed quickly under his own firm guidance, Worcester flashed Eden a sympathetic smile. "You're doing fine, El-tee," he reassured him. "Just fine."

Lieutenant Eden readjusted his rucksack straps, trying to regain his dignity but knowing he was putty in Worcester's hands. To his left, 3rd Squad was moving off single file into the jungle and its assigned mission. Even the confused OCS lieutenant noted the precision and competence of Frantz's men.

It was not the Officer Candidate School precision and competence of close-order drill, crisp uniforms, and short haircuts, but rather the confidence, discipline, and reflexes of true combat professionals. Eden jerked the heavy rucksack back on in a single smooth motion, proud to be associated with such men.

Rechecking his map one more time, Worcester did not notice the lieutenant's movement. When Worcester finally looked up, he was all alone.

God only knew where the Lt. had managed to wander off to. Rather than panic or even curse, Worcester merely pressed his thumb and forefinger against the bridge of his nose. It was the resigned gesture of a man who had been concentrating too hard and been on the job too long but who still had to cope quietly with the incompetence of others. When he heard equipment rattling nearby, he merely squeezed tighter, and smiled to himself.

"We're moving out, lieutenant," he called to the noise.

Third Squad paused briefly just at the edge of the heavier forest to form the correct order of march.

Duffy, the machine gunner, had already removed his shirt and Doc was huffing under the weight of the extra medical supplies he had packed this time. Duffy had the standard towel around his shoulders to keep the rucksack from ripping into his skin. He held the machine gun before him as if it were a small rifle.

McDaniel, beside Doc, kept whispering, "Short" to himself as he gazed into the bush ahead. The stubby M79 grenade launcher looked like another toy in his huge hands.

"I'll take the point," said Frantz as he passed the motley trio.

"Pig on slack," Motown the rifleman called up to Duffy. Motown then trotted up to Frantz's side.

"Don't try to do everything yourself," he warned the squad leader, with a slight nod that indicated that he was volunteering to take the point for him.

"I like point," Frantz said, shrugging. "It breaks the boredom and monotony—"

"Of this tropical paradise," interrupted Motown to finish the thought. Neither man said or showed anything more. They didn't need to.

Frantz proceeded to lead 3rd Squad into a surprisingly thinly wooded gentle grade. He moved smoothly and lithely despite the rucksack. His rifle was poised and bobbing side to side with the movement of his eyes.

The FNGs, on the other hand, were already miserable, stumbling under the weight of their gear. They watched in disbelief as the others marched easily. The others concentrated on the jungle around them, the way they were supposed to, rather than their own misery. The veterans didn't even seem to sweat. They breathed with their mouths closed. Their boots didn't even make a sound as they stepped through the leaves and loose vines that were the jungle floor.

"Shit. These guys know what they're doing," whispered Beletsky in awe.

"Most definitely," confirmed Washburn.

The terrain remained flat and lightly wooded. It was easy and near-ideal humping, with no rain, good visibility, and plenty of cover in case of ambush. The reassuring sounds of squealing lizards, buzzing insects, and distant chattering birds meant that no one else was moving in the area. Frantz was tempted to step up the pace, so as to give his dying FNGs a longer-than-normal break at the first checkpoint.

Soon, however, he heard a faint sound that didn't fit with lizards, bugs, and birds. He didn't know what it was and wasn't even completely certain that he had actually heard it. More than half the things heard or seen in the bush were imaginary. Nonetheless, he froze in a reflexive crouch.

Everyone else automatically froze behind him.

Hearing the noise again, Frantz instinctively pointed his rifle toward it. He did not aim but just pointed, the way Old West gunfighters and duck hunters did: "quick kill" or "instinct firing," they called it back at Fort Campbell, Kentucky.

Ten meters farther down the line of march, Duffy also pointed his machine gun at whatever Frantz had seen or heard.

At the same instant Duffy made his move, everyone else in the line assumed a low crouch, waiting to throw themselves prone and open fire at the slightest provocation.

When the faint sound came again, it was fifteen meters left of where Terry Frantz had first picked it up. This time he caught a glint of metal in the foliage, along with the noise. The glint was no more than twenty meters from his own position. In the same pantherlike motion of throwing himself to the jungle floor, Frantz flicked his M16 to rock and roll, and began firing in short controlled bursts.

Everyone else in the line mimicked the gesture, not knowing yet what they were firing at but relieved to be actually firing, *doing* something, rather than hanging back helplessly in suspense with each forward step taken toward an unknown objective. The frenzy of the firefight itself brought with it a special inner calm that no one who hadn't been there could ever understand and that no one who *had* been there would ever bother to explain.

There it is: it don't mean nothing.

Duffy was methodically spraying the area to the front with his M60 pig, with Gaigin at his side connecting extra belts of ammunition to the one already feeding into the weapon's breech.

Motown lifted his chest to throw a round fragmentation grenade at a sapling tree and then dove back to the ground like John Wayne.

Murphy called loudly but calmly into the radio as the short-timer blood McDaniel pumped high-explosive rounds from his M79 grenade launcher into the tree line. The grenade launcher resembled a sawed-off shotgun—except for the fact that its barrel was about five times as big around as that of a shotgun.

Meanwhile, the FNGs were quickly learning by trial and error how to achieve the rhythm and inner calm of the veterans.

Beletsky fired his first magazine on fully automatic and had to pause to reload again in three seconds. Putting the new magazine in, he swallowed his dry Adam's apple and switched the fire selector switch to semi. He then began firing one round at a time, picking specific targets in the bush—a low-lying twig, an extraordinarily large leaf, a thick vine—even though he could still see no movement or other sign of life.

To Beletsky's right, Bienstock quickly jammed his weapon. To his own surprise, however, he had the composure to take immediate action. He removed the magazine and calmly took out the bullet that had been lodged against the chamber.

He forgot to remove the round already inside the chamber itself, however, and was immediately again out of action. This time he got it right, afraid to even look up at what might be coming toward him as everyone else kept firing. Like Frantz, he began firing in short controlled automatic bursts.

At Bienstock's other flank, Vinnie Languilli had already stopped firing, seeing no point in wasting ammunition on anything he couldn't see. Glancing ahead, he even laughed at the sight of Washburn.

Washburn lay behind a stump and had his face pressed to the ground, with his eyes closed. He had extended the rifle around the corner of his cover and was firing blindly.

No one in the entire squad had yet seen a target.

Frantz's initial instinct was finally confirmed, however, when a wooden-handled Chicom grenade floated toward the line in a low arc. At the same instant, higher-pitched popcornlike cracking of AK-47 rifles joined that of the M16s. The enemy bullets splintered the limbs and sapling trees around 3rd Squad and spat dirt in their faces.

Vinnie Languilli finally began firing with a calm vengeance. He was soon so wrapped up in his work that he didn't notice the black grenadier McDaniel run past him in a crouch.

Firing his grenade launcher with one hand, McDaniel slapped the helmets of Washburn, Bienstock, and Beletsky. Loading another high-explosive round, he motioned for the three FNGs to follow him toward Frantz's position at point. He then ran wildly up toward point, launching his next grenade and reloading as he ran.

Nearer point, just five meters behind Frantz, Duffy and Gaigin were still laying down a steady stream of fire. The machine gun made Duffy's large biceps and pectoral muscles twitter. The barrel was smoking; Gaigin squirted oil onto it from a plastic bottle, to keep it from softening, bending, and dying. The oil sizzled and evaporated as soon as it hit metal.

As McDaniel and the other FNGs threw themselves prone near Frantz, Gaigin motioned for Languilli to run forward with more ammunition for the M60. Each rifleman carried two extra belts of machine-gun rounds in addition to his own basic load of M16 ammunition, for situations like this one. Gaigin was surrounded by mounds of ejected brass shells and gray metal links.

After signaling for the nearest FNG, Gaigin caught another glint of metal in the tree line. He slapped Duffy's sweating shoulder and pointed for him to redirect his fire.

"Two o'clock!" yelled Gaigin. "Again! Short burst! *Eleven* o'clock, *eleven* o'clock . . . *got* him!"

Frantz picked up on the machine-gun crew's target immediately. Under the cover of McDaniel's grenade fire, he ran farther forward and dropped to one knee. Gazing ahead intently, in the direction where Duffy still fired, he loaded a fresh magazine. Then he rose slightly, in a crouch, to spray the entire magazine into whatever Duffy and Gaigin had seen.

A grenade exploded and McDaniel was knocked down. He got up and moved forward but was hit by a bullet. He could tell it was a serious wound but moved forward again and was hit a final time just as he neared the enemy position.

Dropping back again to one knee, Frantz did not realize that McDaniel was gone and that everyone else had stopped firing to watch his own performance.

The FNGs' first firefight was over. It had apparently been a fluke encounter.

Good training for them, Terry Frantz thought, smiling to himself as he looked back. The FNGs had done well. They were still lying prone, with eyes peeled and fingers on the triggers of their weapons. It wouldn't be long before they lost those three derogatory initials.

Less than five minutes after the initial outbreak of violence, 3rd Squad was joined by the headquarters element of the platoon, led by Lieutenant Eden and Platoon Sergeant Worcester. To the lieutenant's surprise, 3rd Squad appeared relaxed rather than on alert.

Nearly everyone else, however, knew the enemy had hightailed it and that there was no need for full alert. Third Squad was safer now, in the aftermath of the firefight while the enemy fled or regrouped, than they would be at any other moment during the entire mission.

Unlike the Americans, Mr. Nathaniel Victor never lingered at the site of battle. He didn't even bother to recover his dead and wounded, let alone try to hold the ground for any tactical or emotional reasons. For Mr. Nathaniel Victor, fighting itself was all that mattered. He had learned over a period of thirty years doing it—first against the Japanese, then the French, now the Americans—when to flee and when to make a stand.

It was almost always best to flee, leaving a few booby traps in your wake.

With the rest of 3rd Squad remaining in the makeshift fighting perimeter, Terry Frantz led Worcester and Lieutenant Eden to the trail where Duffy and Gaigin had finally successfully pinpointed the enemy.

Worcester casually removed three playing cards, all aces of spades, from his breast pocket as Eden stared dumbly at the three bodies that Frantz, Doc, and Motown had collected from the trail and piled together.

"Did you see them?" asked the lieutenant dryly. The lieutenant had never seen corpses before. He was more amazed by the peaceful, almost cherub-like expressions on the dead men's faces than by the callous way his troops treated them. Worcester casually flipped one card onto each man's chest, the symbolic way of tagging them as their unit's kill.

"No," replied Frantz, kneeling. He then reached into the random pile of papers, weapons, ammunition, and gear that had been stripped from the three dead NVA. They had been traveling light, with only one day's ration of rice, but were unusually well armed. Each had carried several Chicom grenades as well as several full magazines of AK-47 rounds. Their clothes were thin and faded but better-tailored and cleaner than the Americans' shapeless jungle fatigues. They looked fresh and professional. Their helmets, however, were shaped like British pith helmets and had no chance of deflecting a grazing round the way the Americans' steel pots could so easily.

Frantz suddenly, triumphantly, pulled a tin canteen from the pile. It was wrapped tightly in a canvas cover, like the Americans' canteens, but made a sloshing noise when he shook it. He shook it back and forth vigorously for the benefit of the green lieutenant.

"Gook, FNG-type," he said with an arrogant smile. "Walking around in the Ashau with half a canteen." He shook it one more time and smiled even broader before adding, "It makes a lot of noise."

Motown, Beletsky, and Bienstock watched Frantz give Lieutenant Eden the lesson from five feet back, from the same position they had taken to give Frantz covering fire. All sense of pride and professionalism had vanished from the two FNGs' faces as they witnessed the demonstration.

Beletsky's cheeks quivered as he removed his own canteen from his pistol belt and sloshed it. It was even louder than the NVA's.

"They should have told us," he mumbled, staring helplessly at the three leaders who knelt over the enemy bodies. He unscrewed the cap and began emptying his canteen into the vine- and root-tangled jungle floor but Motown stopped him, grabbing his wrist and twisting it firmly.

"Put the water into your friends," Motown instructed. "Work together."

Before Beletsky could react to the black man's glaring eyes, Staff Sergeant Frantz reappeared over Bienstock's shoulder.

"We got a blood trail," Frantz informed Motown. "I'll take your bro, Worrier, and the new Alphabet." He glanced casually at Washburn, Beletsky, and Languilli as he ticked off the nicknames he had unconsciously given them. "As you were," he said. Then, he nodded coolly to Washburn. "You're on point," he informed him.

Washburn jumped back and pointed his finger at his own chest, like a little boy unjustly accused of throwing wet toilet paper on the ceiling. "Me?" His voice squeaked in disbelief.

Frantz ignored the stunned face as he inserted a fresh magazine into Washburn's rifle. "There are no friendlies out there," he said to the weapon. He returned the rifle to its owner with a hard slap. "You got a full load," he reminded him.

Terry Frantz had picked Washburn very deliberately. With the Chicano lost, cool soft-spoken Washburn was the best potential leader among the FNGs. He had the sense to know when to be scared and show it but also kept his cool when the others got either overly ecstatic or overly maudlin.

This was a perfect dry run for Washburn. The main NVA element had definitely fled. If there were any wounded in the area who were still able to fire, which Frantz doubted, Washburn had what it took to react.

The squad leader fell in line right behind his reluctant new point man, followed by Languilli and Beletsky. He gave Doc only a slight nod, not wanting to confront his sad eyes, as they walked past him.

Doc was kneeling over the blood grenadier's body at the edge of the perimeter, near the exact spot where McDaniel had taken his position to lay down flanking fire for the white squad leader.

Frantz knew McDaniel had bought the farm but had not bothered to tell the rest of the squad. He knew the veterans had already figured it out, when Doc had run frantically to McDaniel's position but then failed to yell for a medevac bird.

The FNGs, still high from the adrenaline of the firefight, probably didn't even miss McDaniel yet. It wouldn't hit them until a bird was finally brought in to pick up the body.

Despite his own stoicism and his determination to concentrate on the new point man, to make sure *he* didn't buy it, Terry Frantz could not avoid a chill of mixed anguish and anger as he caught Doc filling out the copper-wired field tag from the corner of his eye. Doc was shaking his head almost imperceptibly as he proceeded with his duty, oblivious to the fresh bloodstains he had picked up on his own jungle fatigues.

McDaniel, the short-timer, had died saving Frantz's ass. No one had told him to run up toward the point with the grenade launcher. Nobody should have even expected him to go back into the Ashau, as close as he was to boarding the freedom bird back to the World. McDaniel, so worried about how he would talk and act back in the World, had not complained.

Frantz squeezed his rifle to force himself to refocus on the immediate situation. Washburn was doing fine, following the clots of blood but staying back from the actual trail; checking the vines and limbs for trip wires or springs or grenades with the smooth grace and instinct of a natural point man. Terry Frantz's instinct had once again been correct.

Washburn gestured with the back of his hand before stopping. He then slowly lowered himself to his hands and knees. He crawled forward without even checking to make sure his buddies were crouched behind to cover him. The others remained in a crouch as they followed him.

What Washburn had seen was a bloodstained cartridge belt and canvas-topped NVA pith helmet lying smack in the middle of the trail. After he was certain there were no booby-trap wires and no lingering ambush teams in the surrounding bush, he motioned for Frantz to join him in checking it out.

Frantz lifted the helmet gingerly. Rather than a booby trap grenade or mine, the only things it was hiding were some letters and a stack of black-and-white photographs of a smiling Vietnamese girl. The photos and letters were tucked into the leather sweat band of the helmet liner. The American NCO tossed the photographs aside into the trail's blood clots without even glancing at them and crammed the letters into his leg pocket.

"Where's the body?" asked trembling Beletsky. He whispered loudly; too loud, he himself knew.

"I didn't sign for it," said Languilli, behind him. He said it with the same cool nonchalance with which he had addressed the lost truck driver at the An Lo bridge; as if it were a general's air-conditioned house trailer that was missing rather than a body.

Terry Frantz finally allowed a smile to escape and the FNGs reciprocated instantly.

None of the new men dared to look into their sergeant's eyes, however. The N.C.O.'s eyes were still on duty, still piercing beyond each man and beyond the jungle itself, looking for something that everyone, including himself, knew he would never find.

By the time Frantz nodded for Washburn to lead them back, Washburn's own eyes had already assumed that same blank, piercing, professional gaze.

Before taking his place in line, Beletsky glanced back one more time at the snapshots of the Vietnamese girl. She was smiling and had long black hair. He was tempted to retrieve them and check her out at close range but didn't want to chance the squad leader's wrath. As he refocused on the bobbing rucksack in front of him, it dawned on him how sick his friends back in the World would have thought someone who lusted after the snapshots of a dead man's girl friend. He laughed silently at the absurdity as he followed the rucksacks back into 1st Platoon's makeshift perimeter.

It don't mean nothing, the Worrier thought.

Chapter Nine

That evening, 3rd Squad and the rest of 1st Platoon dug in just a few meters from the site of the fluke afternoon firefight, at the base of the hill known as Dong Ap Bia to the local Vietnamese and numbered 937 on the laminated topographical maps Lieutenant Eden and his squad leaders used to pinpoint their location for Higher. Terry Frantz was the only one in 3rd Squad who knew the hill's number, and even he did not know it had a name. The other enlisted men did not even realize they were near a hill, let alone how steep, high, and potentially strategic it was. They thought they were on a continuing gentle slope, but the tall trees made it impossible to tell how quickly the slope changed.

It was, in fact, one of the highest points between the Ashau Valley's broad network of supply routes and infiltration trails and the Laotian border. It was also gentle enough on three of the four sides to allow either the North Vietnamese or the Americans to bring in heavy machine guns and mortars and even build reinforced semipermanent tunnels, trenches, and fighting bunkers if they wanted to.

For the men of 3rd Squad, such strategic information would have remained irrelevant even if they had known it. In their minds, nobody built anything permanent in the Ashau Valley, nobody would want to lug heavy machine guns and mortars up the slopes and nobody wanted to wage an all-out battle there in the middle of nowhere. Not even the NVA were that masochistic. Everyone was convinced that today's engagement had indeed been a fluke and that nothing else would be found.

Everyone, that was, except Staff Sergeant Terry Frantz. The three dead men's fresh uniforms and unusually large supply of ammunition stayed with him all afternoon. You didn't find troops equipped that well unless they were part of a larger element. Mr. Nathaniel Victor didn't waste spare ammunition on small ambush units who could do the job of harassing and scaring the Americans with just one magazine.

That evening, the troops of 3rd Squad were still high from the firefight. They had lost only one of their own and had wasted at least three and probably more of the enemy. A score like that was as close as many units ever came to tangible victory over the enemy. Their thoughts were not on the ammunition Terry Frantz had found or the prospect of climbing the hill known as Dong Ap Bia.

Although they went about professionally preparing cover and lines of fire against the ambush and sapper teams that *might* arrive with the blanket of darkness (a long shot), their thoughts vacillated between the most immediate concerns and the longest-range dreams.

The immediate concerns were such issues as getting the caked foot powder out of the tiny holes in the can, finding somebody who hadn't used all his insect repellant and was willing to share, deciding which of the twelve standard C-ration menus to indulge in, and trying to avoid the midnight-to-two-o'clock shift of guard duty and radio watch. The long-range dreams were the girl back home, the new car, and all that cash that would be waiting in the bank. The nest egg ranged from ninety dollars a month for a buck private to more than three hundred a month for staff sergeants like Terry Frantz, plus the sixty-five a month every man got regardless of rank as a "hostile fire" bonus.

None of them thought of McDaniel or Galvan or even where they were and what they were *really* doing there. They were just passing through, counting the days and trying to do the job as best they could in order to get by and get out. Had the country itself been transported to any other part of the world, and had they visited in civilian clothes and slept in hotel beds, they would have been awestricken by the raw spectacular beauty that surrounded them every moment of every day: the bold sunsets and sunrises against the endless cloud-shrouded mountain ridges; the geometrical precision and delicateness of the rice paddies carved into the slopes; the straight two-hundred-foot-tall teakwood trees and the countless varieties of flora and fauna at their feet.

In their present circumstances, however, there was no time to contemplate the beauty God had wrought or to thank him for the privilege of being allowed to behold it. Any thanks given to God were for allowing someone *else* to be the one to catch the sniper's round or step on the mine or booby trap. Flora and fauna were good for camouflage and teakwoods made good defilade cover, but all of them were pretty much useless against mortars, rockets, red ants, centipedes, and bunker rats.

Third Squad's sector of the perimeter faced the very blood trail where Beletsky had chosen to leave the enemy's snapshots behind. Each man dug a shallow fighting hole just wide and long enough for his own body. They then split off in pairs, with each pair erecting a low sleeping hooch near the fighting holes. To build the hooch, they snapped two ponchos together and stretched them over a low frame of bamboo. They put their air mattresses inside the hooches but didn't blow them up, for fear that the squeaking noise during the night might startle a nervous enemy or even a friendly troop on guard duty. After everyone's position was set, Frantz made the rounds to distribute extra ammunition and grenades.

As usual, the RTO Murphy and the machine-gun team of Duffy and Gaigin were trying to get in one more full hand of cards.

Doc and Motown sat together jiving. They seemed to be making an extra effort to sound cool and hip, with the conspicuous absence of McDaniel.

Beletsky was writing CLAIRE on the cloth camouflage cover of his steel helmet with a ballpoint pen, while Bienstock worked on his short-timer's calendar.

The short-timer's calendar, showing how many days to DEROS—Date of Estimated Rotation to States—was as much a part of most grunts' gear as were their socks and ammunition. Most men constantly tried to outdo themselves and one another in making the calendar as elaborate as possible. Some made them in the shape of women's bodies, with 1 at the vagina; others made maps of the United States and put the magic 1 in their hometown.

Bienstock was doing his in the format of a normal calendar, with neat straight rows of days and dates. He was using four different colored pens: one for his own count, one for Beletsky, one for Languilli, and one for Washburn. He was doing it on a piece of cardboard he had ripped from a C-ration carton.

"October one-niner and we'll have been here six months," he announced longingly. "That's halfway. I'm marking that in blue. I got different-colored pens for each of us. Washburn got here the same day as us, didn't he?"

Beletsky nodded without looking up from his own artwork. "And that other guy and Alphabet the day before," he added.

Bienstock said, "Okay. Thanks."

Languilli's eyes jerked up from the automobile sales brochures he was perusing. He still had not adapted to the Alphabet moniker, even though he was no longer offended by it.

"*Short,*" Languilli boasted to the others. The word *short,* meaning the speaker had less time to go than whomever he was addressing, was the GI's ultimate boast in Vietnam.

Languilli then turned to Frantz with his brochures, which he had carried with him in the rucksack from base camp. "Check this out . . . I love this Camaro," he said.

Frantz knew that cars were not what was really on the soldier's mind.

"We did good today," the Italian finally said, with the tone of a schoolboy begging the teacher's approval. "We got our cherry busted, didn't we, Sarge?"

Frantz glowered. "One of my people got killed," he reminded the cocky FNG. "That's all that happened today."

Even that philosophical reminder did not seem to dampen the FNGs' determination to block out their actual situation.

"Double-digit midget," announced Bienstock as he marked the milestone 99 on his cardboard calendar. He studied the work of art at arm's length, like a critic. "It's a lifetime," he muttered.

Beletsky too paused to study his own handiwork after finishing the E in Claire. "There it is," he proclaimed, satisfied with himself.

Terry Frantz could not help smile again at their innocence and youth. Before any of them could detect his emotion, however, he turned his head toward Doc and Motown, sitting five feet away, in front of their poncho hooch.

To Frantz's surprise, Doc was already staring directly at him. From the hot look in his eyes, he had been doing so for some time. The medic was giving him that glare of mixed self-pity, pride, and hatred: that same glare that had caused Frantz to wonder how Doc would hold up the next time they ran into real shit.

"You knew that man wasn't going to slack off because he was short," Doc told him. His voice grew stronger with each word, drawing the rest of the squad's attention even though he still had the sense to keep it at a near-whisper to avoid tempting any snipers that might be gulping their rice nearby.

"You *knew* the brother was going to do his job," said the medic, eulogizing his friend.

Terry Frantz gritted his teeth to hold in his temper. He knew as well as Doc that McDaniel had bought it while covering for him. But Frantz himself would have done the same thing for McDaniel or any other member of 3rd Squad, and Doc knew it. Doc knew damned well he couldn't have kept McDaniel back from the CA just because he was short. Doc was just letting off steam.

"Why didn't *you* put him on profile?" challenged Frantz to the trembling black man.

"Because he was one healthy individual," answered the medic, spontaneously, not even realizing he was using the same logic the squad leader himself would have. "I got people in this platoon who are so fucking sick they wouldn't be allowed in a hospital," Doc added, "but out here they have to 'ruck up, move out, and press on.' "

Frantz had made his point and did not want to rub it in. Doc had more right than most to blow off steam. McDaniel had been a friend as well as a blood.

As Doc settled back in a Vietnamese squat, bad Motown put another Temptations tape into his cassette player. Motown knew even better than Frantz that Doc needed to let it out. Motown now covered his buddy's ass with the music to divert the honkies' attention away from him. The music was "I Wish It Would Rain." He said, "Don't mean nothing, Doc . . . Not a thing . . . Come on, soul. You owe it to yourself."

Doc slowly started to clap, his anger, frustration, and tension channeling into the movements.

Motown said, "There it is, Doc."

As if on cue, the new blood Washburn approached as soon as the notes began. Washburn was returning from a defecation mission at the edge of the perimeter, with rifle in one hand and entrenching tool and toilet paper in the other. He began bobbing to the rhythm of the music as he walked.

"Look at that brother move, Doc," said Motown. "Did you *see* him on point today?" He craned his neck to the sheepish Georgian's face. "Walk point, brother," he commanded. "Walk point."

Washburn crouched and began waving his rifle and entrenching tool side to side in rhythmic mockery of the classic point man's stance, stepping in time with the music.

A proud and satisfied smile had replaced the bitterness in Doc's face. ''The 'Brothers' are back,'' he announced to the rest of the squad. ''We have 'Pointman,' 'Motown on slack,' and yours truly, 'Bag 'em, Tag 'em, and Forget 'em.' It don't mean nothing, man. Not a thing.'' All three black men began miming the words to the cassette player's song.

That was the way emotions ran in the jungle: the most savage fury would fade to complete peace and harmony and then transform back to fury with the drop of the right or wrong word or the right or wrong shift in the wind.

It didn't mean nothing, as the troops knew.

Terry Frantz again smiled proudly. The weird group may have looked like childish clowns or worse to someone in the suburbs back in the World, but as far as he was concerned at that moment, they were the very best his country and even the whole damned fucking human race could ever hope to produce.

The squad leader rose and moved quietly away from both groups—whites and bloods—to avoid again detracting from their innocence. He stood by a tree near the center of the perimeter, gazing up at the silhouetted branches and leaves. He noticed, finally, that the air was cool and fresh. Birds were still chirping and a monkey was howling somewhere in the distance. The monkey's shriek echoed through the valley like a yodeler's song might have in the less spectacular and less exotic Swiss Alps.

As usual, the squad leader's musing was soon interrupted. Worcester joined him, but did not seem to notice what he had been gazing at.

"We got McDaniel's body out on the Charlie-Charlie bird," announced the platoon sergeant.

This was not news to Frantz. Every troop in the perimeter had seen the colonel's bubble-canopied loach—LOH, light observation helicopter, "loach" to the grunts—come and go. The colonel, who called himself Blackjack on the radio, had brought in his Command and Control (Charlie-Charlie) bird to drop off new maps and radio codes for Lieutenant Eden. The Old Man had graciously taken the black grenadier's plastic-shrouded body back out with him.

"All he wanted to do was go home in his jump boots and his medals," Frantz told the filtered stars, rather than his friend. "He couldn't believe they'd call him a jerk—"

"And worse, worse," interrupted Worcester, his tone now 100 percent sympathetic. Unlike last night, this was the appropriate time to vent a little self-pity. Worcester himself had already returned to the World, once. He had learned firsthand the bitter lesson that the grunt was better understood and respected by Mr. Nathaniel Victor than by the rest of his own generation, and had fled back to the army and Vietnam.

Worcester hoped his friend would continue with more epithets, hoped he would go ahead and let it *all* out of his system for at least one moment. Frantz, however, had already gone sullen again, gazing at the mostly hidden sky.

"People get hurt out here," Worcester himself finally said.

"Don't tell me he died for God, Country, and the 101st Airborne Division." The bitterness was back, full force, stunning Worcester.

"I'd never say that shit to anybody." It was now Worcester's turn to let off steam, even though he didn't realize it. "McDaniel didn't 'die' for anything. He didn't leave his goddam guts on a goddam trail in the goddam Ashau Valley for a medal, hometown, or any of that shit. He *flanked* that automatic weapon, and took it out, for *you*. And for the Third Squad. Don't you give them anything less."

Terry Frantz calmly pulled a C-ration cigarette from the tiny package tucked into the band holding his camouflage cover tight to his steel pot. Cupping the match's flame with his hand, he shared the smoke with his brother staff sergeant. "When we get out of this valley, Worcester," he told him sympathetically, "I *am* going to kick your ass."

"There it is," said Lieutenant Eden's right arm and guardian angel, grinning innocently.

After the cigarette, Frantz followed the other sergeant to the command post position in the center of the perimeter. Lieutenant Eden and RTO Murphy were kneeling with the other three squad leaders in a circle.

Frantz had forgotten there was to be a briefing on today's action and the next phase. He suddenly realized that was the reason Worcester had come to him at the tree. He was now doubly thankful Worcester had taken the time to talk and smoke.

Several PRC-25 radios were spread amidst the group, each monitoring a different command frequency. Only Murphy paid any attention to the radios' traffic, however; the others looked intently at a map spread on the ground.

Murphy was calling in grids for defensive targets, "Delta Tangos," to the mortar and artillery batteries several hills away while the others waited patiently for the lieutenant to say something.

"Cold Steel, this is One Six Alpha," Murphy muttered into his handset in a flat mechanical tone. "Prepare to copy, over."

"This is Cold Steel, over."

"Delta Tango for Red One Six . . . " Murphy's voice droned on in the background.

The lieutenant remained silent. It appeared that without the props of Pentagon forms to distribute to the men, he didn't know how to begin. The squad leaders darted nervously to and from one another's eyes.

Worcester finally knelt at the lieutenant's side and stared coldly at each of the other N.C.O.s, as if he had been ordered by the lieutenant to shut them down and save what little dignity he had left. "Battalion wants us to go back to where Frantz made contact today," he reported, easily drowning out the radio chatter and ignoring the mum lieutenant. "They say there are some stragglers left on this position—here." He jabbed his finger into a tight ring of concentric oval lines on the map. "Hill 937."

With the mention of the word *stragglers,* Terry Frantz was suddenly even more indignant than he had been when fantasizing about kicking some college students' asses. "Those KIAs were clean and well equipped," he contradicted his friend. "They *weren't* stragglers."

Lieutenant Eden's eyes suddenly perked up, as if coming out of a trance. He gave 3rd Squad's impudent N.C.O. the same incredulous steel stare he would have given a soldier back in basic training who claimed he couldn't march on Sundays because of religious conviction. "Military Intelligence says there are no organized NVA elements in this AO," he told Frantz.

AO stood for "area of operation." Terry Frantz knew Lieutenant Eden couldn't have found his way either into or out of this AO even if it were marked with flares every five meters. "Military Intelligence could fuck up a wet dream," he told him. *"Sir."*

"All right, man," implored Worcester, intervening to save Frantz from his own candor. "Hold on. We're on the same side here. Tomorrow we'll just get our people quietly off this hill, Recon 937, *then* we'll call in a log bird for hot chow and clean socks." He stared coldly into the lieutenant's eyes. "Isn't that right, Lieutenant?"

"Roger that," replied the officer with no hesitation.

"Murphy is calling in H and I and Delta Tangos," continued Worcester. "The GTL will run over the November side. Internal and external freaks are same-same. Squad leaders, make sure your people have dry feet, clean water, salt pills, and beaucoup ammo." He glanced warily at Frantz. "Just in case," he mumbled in a lower voice, motioning at the same time that the briefing was over. "That's all."

Frantz and Worcester lingered beside the lieutenant for a few seconds more, looking at each other with knowing Open Grave eyes. Murphy was still calling in his harassment and interdiction and defensive targets on the radio.

Frantz returned to the 3rd Squad area and announced, "Gather round. Listen up. Zero eight hundred hours, we are going back in."

Chapter Ten

Terry Frantz did not sleep at all that night. After he had pulled his first shift of radio watch—N.C.O.s passed their normal nighttime waking hours monitoring the radio rather than pulling perimeter guard—he did not bother to awaken Murphy for his turn. He could not get the three dead NVAs' full magazines, clean clothes, and missing rucksacks out of his mind. They were *not* stragglers, and Worcester fucking-A *knew* it. Even the green lieutenant should have known it. How could *anybody* end up where they had found them—with no gear other than ammunition and weapons, and with just a day's rations—if they weren't part of a larger element based nearby?

His buddy Worcester knew all the men of 1st Platoon were in for real shit soon, but had not had the balls to argue with the lieutenant or anyone higher. Worcester was playing the lifer game after all, Frantz was convinced. Worcester had found a home and didn't want to make waves. Even if it meant letting a few grunts get blown away by Mr. Nathaniel Victor.

He wanted to roust both Worcester and the lieutenant and kick the shit out of them but instead passed the time lying helplessly beside the PRC-25, staring up at the brilliant stars shining above the foliage of the Ashau Valley's triple canopy jungle.

In the morning, he joined the other squad leaders in rousting the men of 1st Platoon before dawn. As usual, a heavy mist and fog covered the entire area. Even though there had been no rain, everyone awoke soaked. The poncho hooches were useless against the ubiquitous mist. The wetness in turn made the rucksacks even heavier and tempers even more short-fused.

No one had had more than two uninterrupted hours of sleep. No one bothered to shave. Everyone was by now immune to the stench and filth of each other.

The hoarseness of the usual morning coughs and gripes about no sleep and bad food echoed from the perimeter up toward the hidden hill. The flat depressing noise of the men's voices, however, was only a faint symptom of the apprehension writhing in each one's mind. Everyone knew they would be moving out for the so-called mop-up operation that Platoon Sergeant Worcester had so weakly said would be just a quick reconnoiter and then a helicopter ride back to base camp. Everyone tried desperately to believe that was what it *would* be. Like Terry Frantz, however, everyone had a hard time swallowing it. Especially the men of 3rd Squad who had inadvertently stumbled into the whole mess. If that damned stupid NVA hadn't let his canteen slosh yesterday, who knew where they might be headed this morning? Maybe even back to Mama-san's whorehouse near the An Lo bridge.

Murphy made his final radio check to Higher with everyone else in the squad milling around him, anxious for the signal to move up the hill and get it over with. "Chief, this is Rover One," he called into the black plastic handset. "Commo check, over."

The men's eyes focused unconsciously on the flexible antenna protruding from Murphy's ruck as Higher acknowledged: "Rover. Chief. Lazy Crazy. Ho Chi Minh." The antenna folded like a carpenter's measuring rule, in twelve-inch sections, but also bent easily under any foliage or other obstacle.

"Same-same," replied Murphy. "Thank you much." He slapped the telephonelike handset into the hook on his ruck strap, at his right breast.

Worcester and Frantz lingered over a canteen cup of coffee at the edge of the perimeter as they awaited the exact second for moving the men out. In the insane yin and yang ebb and flow of emotion and rationality that was Vietnam, Frantz had forgotten the anger of last night. It was too late to do any arguing or change anything, as Worcester himself had known last night. Frantz was again glad he would have the cool and highly skilled Worcester behind him this morning.

"What are you doing today?" asked Frantz, to break the maddening silence as everyone in the area huddled nervously under their bulging rucksacks.

"I'm going to grab a six-pack, put the top down, and take a ride with my darling."

"Why not?" nodded Frantz. "Vietnam is—"

"The fun capital of the world," said Worcester, finishing the cliché.

Worcester hung back and toasted with the canteen cup when Terry Frantz finally led 3rd Squad up the hill. He knew they could be headed for the real thing today, but he also knew he would be right behind them. This was what they were paid for, after all.

Besides, Worcester told himself, 3rd Squad's assignment was, on paper at least, one of the easiest of all the units now moving in the area. They were to hang back near the base of a lower hill off to the side of Hill 937 while 3rd Platoon made a classic on-line infantry assault to reconnoiter the objective by fire.

It was to be a textbook operation; the kind of operation that brought wet dreams to old-school regular infantry battalion commanders like Blackjack. Blackjack and his peers had made their careers as junior officers in World War II and Korea and still longed for those days of large-scale tactical maneuver and battle, rather than the small-unit, hit-or-miss ambushes and raids more typical of Vietnam.

Blackjack now hovered above the hill in his command-and-control loach, anxious to begin directing what he hoped against all odds would develop into a real battle.

Small arms fire was already audible in the distance beneath the whining and slapping of the helicopter's turbine and rotors as 3rd Squad moved out. Oblivious to the background noise, they moved quickly through the flat wooded area of yesterday's encounter with the NVA. Despite the easy walking, however, the men's jungle fatigues were immediately further drenched with fresh sweat as well as mist.

Frantz's own warning last night now returned with a chill. They *definitely* hadn't been stragglers. Stragglers would have hightailed at the sight of the loach, and Blackjack knew it. The lifers were jerking the grunts' chains once again, and Frantz knew it. It made him fighting mad—which was exactly the way the lifers wanted him to be.

Frantz knelt next to Worcester, Murphy and the squad leaders from 1st and 2nd squads, Myers and Smitty. Eden was staying in the background and observing as Worcester talked on the radio and did the briefing.

"Red Six, One Six Charlie, over."

"This is Red Six, over" came over the radio.

"One Six Charlie preparing to assault three zero north of phase line Alpha, over."

"Roger that."

Worcester turned to Frantz and said, "We're getting titi small arms from up there. Blackjack wants us to mop up any stragglers. First and Second squads will move out from here. I want you to move your people into a flanking position." He then spoke to the group and said, "Let's make believers out of these sorry-assed bastards. Move it."

Myers and Smitty joined their squads and started up the hill. Frantz led his squad towards a flanking position.

As Beletsky tripped on the rough ground he spoke his complaint: "This isn't the plan we worked out, man. We're supposed to be going up the other hill."

Motown looked up and eyed the circling command helicopter. "It's the same old shit, man—the man in the bird wants to play war."

Suddenly, they heard the crackle of AK-47 fire and dove to the ground. The fire was not directed at them, however. At the point of the main advance, Myers's lifeless body had fallen on top of the wounded radioman who was using it as a shield against the automatic-weapons fire that was concentrating on him.

Small-arms and rocket fire tore into 1st Platoon and pinned them down. Smitty and six of his men lay out in the open, wounded.

Murphy was now in contact with the commander. "Red Six, One Six Alpha, heavy contact, over," he yelled.

The only reply was, "One Six Alpha, keep me advised, over."

Worcester acted quickly and decisively. "Frantz, move your people." He then turned to Murphy and said, "Push in on Third Platoon's internal and get them to mark their forward positions for Cold Steel."

Frantz quickly and authoritatively got his men into action. As they reached the men under attack, he took note of the wounded troopers strewn over the open field and determined where the bulk of the enemy fire was coming from. He called out, "Duffy, take your weapon forward," pointing to a spot, "and lay your covering fire *over* over our friend-lies."

Languilli instinctively went with Duffy and his second man, Gaigin. They crouched as they ran with canteens, bandoliers of ammunition and dog tags bouncing against their bodies. Bullets were zipping by just over their heads. Languilli crouched even lower and ran ahead of the other two. With the whizzing bullets leaving a gust of breeze in their wake, he suddenly knew what the expression "scared shitless" really meant.

With his machine-gun team setting up, Frantz ran to Beletsky and said, "Put your rounds seventy-five meters out."

As Beletsky dutifully began fumbling with the grenade launcher's folding sight mechanism, Frantz jerked the weapon out of his hands. Without looking at the sight, he fired a round of high explosive with a hollow *thup*—not unlike the *thup* of an enemy .60 millimeter mortar.

"That's where I want it," he informed Beletsky as he returned the weapon to him.

Duffy opened up with the big M60 machine gun, and everyone else joined in the firing. Frantz yelled out, "Motown, get your goddam people moving."

Motown turned to Bienstock and said, "Bieny, come on," and the two of them started to run and fire.

As medics started to race over the field tending to the wounded, white marker smoke popped on the hill in front of Frantz and then artillery rounds from their fire mission started to impact beyond the smoke in the area where the enemy fire had been coming from.

Murphy yelled into the radio, "Blow the shit out of them."

The only reply from the artillery location was a calm voice that said, "Use proper radio procedure, over."

The FNG, Bienstock, had no trouble reloading his weapon this time. He laid down covering fire so that Doc could crawl forward toward Myers's twisted body.

After quickly confirming that Myers had bought it, the black medic strained with all his might to pull the wounded RTO out from under the dead body. The 3rd Platoon RTO was still alive but in deep shock. He stared steadily and calmly at the sky as Doc dragged him back to the relative safety of 3rd Squad, 1st Platoon's position.

Chapter Eleven

The history books would later officially record the naïve on-line assault as the opening salvo in the Battle for Hill 937.

The staccato sounds of small arms fire and the deep explosions of artillery continued echoing through the valley the rest of the day. Third Squad, 1st Platoon, stayed in the same position where they had covered 3rd Platoon's withdrawal. No one fired his weapon again, however, after Doc's return with the dazed and useless RTO. The enemy was also either gathering his wounded, regrouping, or redirecting his fire to elements working independently of Bravo Company. Third Squad didn't worry about the small arms and artillery coming from somewhere else on the hill, even though it meant the operation had already become far more than anyone back at base camp had planned yesterday morning. They lay almost leisurely at their assigned positions, with nothing to do as the stragglers and walking wounded continued to file by.

Each man's real priority was not to scan the terrain for the enemy but to avoid the drawn and bleeding faces and voices of their passing comrades. Few things were more demoralizing than a file of dazed walking wounded. Not even the dead were so demoralizing; you could look away from the gaping eyes of the dead and they wouldn't follow you.

The men of 3rd Squad tried to pass the time by counting the bullets in their bandoliers and watching the ants and mosquitoes maneuver around them. It was a good time to take that weekly antimalaria pill—the big orange "shitter" pill.

At five o'clock, they were finally ordered back down to the site where they had dug in the previous evening; the site near the near-extinguished blood trail where they had unknowingly scored the first three KIAs of the battle, which had now become the central medical evacuation point for all American units operating on or around Hill 937.

The original impromptu perimeter had grown to three times the size of last night and had been completely stripped of vegetation, to make the medevac helicopters' arrival and departure as quick and safe as possible. Each time a bird came in, everyone in the area ducked and pressed his steel pot tightly to his head. There was no protection, however, against the stinging bits of torn clothing, filthy battle dressings, and splintered ammo crates kicked up by the rotors' backwash.

As evening approached, some men tried to catch a nap before the darkness forced them to 100 percent alert status, with no one allowed to sleep. Others cleaned their weapons, snacked on C-ration peanut butter and crackers, or wrote letters back to the World.

None of them was able to concentrate very long on whatever activity he had chosen. If the disruption wasn't the helicopters, it was the continuous groans, cries, and stares of the latest wounded waiting to be lifted out or the loud rumbling of incoming artillery rounds a few hundred meters up the hill.

Worcester and Frantz again lingered apart from the rest of 3rd Squad, near a cluster of randomly piled wooden ammo crates. When the inevitable evening rain began falling, lightly and even soothingly at first, Worcester bit into a dead cigar stub that had been in his mouth for hours. He did not speak. His only gesture was to run his hand across his coarse stubble beard, as if trying futilely to remember the last time he'd had a hot shave and a less-than-six-month-old cigar.

As the rain continued, both men turned to the drumming sound of water against rubber. It was the rain splashing off a neat row of zipped-up body bags that were awaiting evacuation.

"Have you heard from the old lady?" asked Frantz, trying to act as if the sight and sound had no effect.

"Never happen," answered Worcester, also with no apparent emotion.

The two combat leaders said no more. There was nothing else that either needed to be said or could be said as they waited for the darkness and whatever it might bring down from the hill. They remained standing side by side, oblivious to the rain falling on them but unable to escape the *tap, tap, tap* coming from the black rubber body bags behind them.

Fortunately, there was a half-moon and no clouds that evening. Everyone in the perimeter was able to distinguish everything clearly.

Nonetheless, flares were sent into the sky at regular intervals. The flares were for the psychological benefit of the Americans. If the sappers *really* wanted to move in, no amount of illumination would deter them.

Beletsky was enthralled by the parachutes and the squeaking noise the flares made as they floated and descended. They reminded him of the cheap plastic toy Batman parachutes he used to get in Crackerjack boxes, which never worked. He wondered how the army did it as he glanced at Languilli stirring the hot chocolate. He and Languilli were squatting over a C-ration stove and monitoring the radio as Murphy worked the calls.

"Remember in basic?" asked Beletsky, still studying the flares. "How they told us to cover an eye in case a flare goes so that we don't lose our night vision?"

"They said that," muttered Languilli reluctantly, staring into the hot chocolate as he prepared for another of Worrier's quizzes.

"Do you think it matters which eye you cover? Do you want your good eye for the flare? Or do you want it for the night vision?"

Languilli struggled to control his temper. "Beletsky, do you stay awake at night thinking of things you should worry about?"

"Do you think maybe we should ask?"

Giving up, Languilli shook his head and smiled warmly at his friend. Beletsky continued staring intently, waiting for an answer and failing to see the humor of the situation.

"What are you guys doing here?" asked Staff Sergeant Frantz.

Both men jumped back. The staff sergeant was just two feet away, standing over them and pointing at their PRC-25, but they hadn't even heard him approach. They had no idea how long he had been hovering above them. Han, the grease-bodied Vietnamese infiltration expert, could not have done a better job ambushing them.

"We're just having some hot chocolate," Beletsky said.

"Anything?" Frantz asked Murphy.

"Nothing," said Murphy. "I came up on the Delta Darlings' push. Same-same, negative sitrep. It looks like we're getting out of here tomorrow."

"Do you want some hot chocolate?" asked Languilli.

To their surprise, he did. He did not bother to thank them at first, however. "Try the bullshit net," he ordered Murphy as he took the cup. After the first sip—after a long pause, as if judging the flavor at a county fair—he turned to the man who had freaked out over being unable to remember the Chicano's first name. "Thank you much," he told him in a complimentary tone that made even Languilli nervous.

"What's the bullshit net?" asked Beletsky, missing all nuances as usual.

With his face again stern and emotionless, Frantz leaned forward and took the PRC-25 himself. As soon as he began turning the knob to change frequencies, Murphy snapped to.

"Are we getting out of here tomorrow?" asked Languilli, sensing incorrectly from the squad leader's earlier smile that this might be a good time for everyone to level with each other. He asked it desperately, shamelessly.

Are we getting out of here tomorrow?

That had been the question on every mind since digging in at the edge of the gruesome medevac area. Cool Vinnie Languilli was the first one with the balls to actually ask it out loud.

"Definitely," lied Frantz, retreating from the two soldiers' eyes to the hot chocolate at his side. Frantz knew that Motown had been right this morning: Blackjack wanted to play war. There was more than stragglers at the top of that hill and Blackjack would not call back a single man until he knew exactly what and who it was. Blackjack wanted a nice body count to report to Division. All lieutenant colonels needed all the nice body counts they could get in punching their cards for promotion to general.

The artificially broad and thin smile on the staff sergeant's face frightened Languilli. "I am going straight to the PX and ordering the Firebird," he said abruptly, hoping to end the conversation.

"What happened to the Camaro?" asked Frantz calmly, as if they had been talking cars all along. He remembered times with his father when they argued over the use of the car, or enjoyed washing it together, or, further back, when he was just a kid and they'd go for a drive and his dad would let him "steer" the wheel. "My dad won't drive anything but a Buick," he added after a pause.

Even Beletsky was now frightened by the squad leader's weird smile. It was the irrational and oblivious smile of someone on a drug trip. Beletsky knew Frantz didn't do drugs, which only made it scarier.

Frantz continued adjusting the radio, staring at the knob as if in a trance. The three dead NVAs' shining full magazines had once again blocked all else from his brain. He could not remember the last time he had slept: and he did not *want* to sleep.

"Hanoi Hanna. She has the best sounds in the valley," said Murphy, tuning in the enemy frequency. "And, oh boy, she *does* have a rap: 'We love you too much, drop your weapons, Uncle Ho will give you a water buffalo and your own rice paddy to shit in.' Sometimes they get *American* assholes to tell us what assholes we are. No lie. It's a trip." The transmission was static-filled and broken.

"American soldiers and marines," Hanoi Hanna was saying, "embrace the heroic people of Vietnam like many of your heroic countrymen . . ."

Languilli lit a cigarette and began smoking through cupped hands, the way they had said you could back at Fort Bragg, North Carolina. He did not know what hit him as Terry Frantz flew on top of him, knocking him down into his fighting hole before he had even taken a full draw.

"The rock pile," Hanoi Hanna was saying. "Why fight the heroic People's Army while your own government betrays you and the heroic American friends of Vietnam?"

"If you have to smoke at night," Frantz told the FNG, in a calm but menacing half-whisper, "put a poncho over your head."

"And I would like to send this special dedication to the Screaming Eagles in the Ashau Valley," purred Hanna.

"I had my hands cupped over it," argued Languilli.

Rather than waste words, Terry Frantz picked up the still-burning cigarette and bent over in the hole, squeezing Languilli. He cupped his hands tightly around it before taking a drag. The red light seeped out both hands, an easy target for even a dumb FNG.

"You may be killed any time," warned Hanna, "day or night. Like your shadow, Death is following you everywhere."

The crazed squad leader was grinning evilly at Languilli.

It was all, finally, more than Beletsky could take. The crazy radio bitch's jibberish; Staff Sergeant Terry Frantz's slinking and his goddam *knowing* everything, all the time. And now, his doper grin. How were you supposed to *act?*

"How am I supposed to know all this shit?" he blurted. "Ponchos over your head, no half-canteens, dog tags on the boots, carry the Claymore detonator when setting them up." Without realizing it, Beletsky was off on his own tirade; one that would have looked just as weird, just as drug-induced, as the staff sergeant's performance would have to an untrained eye back in the World.

"Booby traps in the ham and lima motherfuckers, orange pills once a week, whites daily-daily. Don't walk on trails. You can smell a gook. Food in the sock, halazone in the water. Secure your frags, don't scratch the ringworm. And Charlie can see at night, crawl through the concertina. And he pisses napalm." He pointed to the static-filled radio. "And now this bullshit and all the time *I'm* worrying I might forget something!"

The FNG whirled to Frantz but the inhuman N.C.O. had disappeared into the night, as quickly and magically as he had appeared.

Chapter Twelve

With the squad leader's disappearance, Beletsky finally shut up for the night. But the frustration that had launched his own babbling sermon only grew worse with the forced silence.

Fucking Frantz is too smart and too cool to be human, he thought to himself as he crawled into the low pancho hooch he shared with Languilli.

All the old-timers were too damn cool, he thought. The jungle had made them abnormal, made them boony freaks, and they didn't even realize it. How were you supposed to *act* among such freaks?

The questions kept churning in Beletsky's mind all night, depriving him any sleep. During his guard shift, he kept mumbling the same questions to himself. "How am I supposed to know? How am I supposed to act?"

The more he tried to forget the questions, the more new ones emerged in their place. Returning to the hooch, he gazed helplessly at the mud that seemed almost translucent through the open crack at the bottom of the stretched poncho. The mosquitoes were buzzing like Japanese dive bombers in old World War II movies and the ants were marching in rout-step circles. The ants seemed dazed, somebody must have either mortared them or made them listen to Hanoi Hanna.

He was still staring at the mud when other troops in the platoon began rucking up and Blackjack's Charlie-Charlie loach began slapping in from the south with the crack of dawn. Peering out of the hooch, he realized that the rest of 3rd Squad was already breaking camp. Other units—entire platoons as well as squads—were already rucked up and moving in single file for another ascent on Hill 937. Languilli, his hooch-mate, had managed to slip out without his even realizing it, like Frantz had last night.

Just ten feet away, Terry Frantz was now barking orders as he tried to get 3rd Squad organized and motivated for the day.

"Okay! On your feet, people," he ordered. "Wake up. It's time to earn your combat pay."

"I thought we were pulling off this hill. Today," argued Beletsky as he watched the other elements move out. He was disgusted by the N.C.O.'s completely normal, undrugged expression and manners.

"Don't think," Motown told him coolly, defending the mad leader.

"Hey, Motown, fuck you," said Beletsky defiantly.

Nobody even seemed to hear Worrier's bold remark, let alone take it seriously. Everyone but Beletsky himself was busily and professionally repacking his bedroll or checking his weapon. They were all bantering lightheartedly, as if this were nothing more than a Boy Scout camping exercise.

"I need goddam boots, Sarge," grumbled Gaigin.

"My aching back," groaned Duffy as he bent and lifted the big M60.

"My whole fucking body hurts," chimed in mellow-voiced Washburn.

"My dick hurts," added Bienstock.

None of them, not even Beletsky, had noticed the complacency fade from their squad leader's face. Normally, Frantz would have bitched right along with them. Now, however, he was flitting his eyes nervously from one man to the next. He stood impatiently with his hands on his hips, tapping his fingers on the two ammo pouches clipped to his pistol belt.

"Then drop ten and beat it," he finally told Bienstock, offering him the cupped jerking-off gesture with his left hand. He addressed the entire squad: "I don't want to hear any more of this shit. You get your heads out of your asses! Blackjack wants us to take this hill."

"What's he going to do with it?" interrupted Doc, hoping to cool him down.

"Pave it and turn it into a goddam parking lot," mumbled the embarrassed squad leader. "Now *move* out."

Doc let it drop. The man was suffering from no sleep and bad nerves, like everybody else. Frantz would be okay once he got back in the bush.

Mortar rounds were already exploding far to the front as the men of 3rd Squad, 1st Platoon, Bravo Company, lunged forward in one final effort to get the rucksacks as high and evenly balanced on their shoulders as possible and minimize both the weight and the cutting of the straps against their flesh.

Small arms fire was also erupting sporadically as they moved out single file.

The fire seemed to intensify with each step, though it still wasn't directed at 3rd Squad and no one yet had any idea which other friendly elements were involved. As the radio's traffic quickly became more frantic, however, it was soon obvious that nearly all of Bravo Company was involved in the fighting in one manner or another—either taking enemy fire directly or firing support for whoever was.

As 3rd Squad continued up the hill, they could actually see fire teams from other squads and platoons falling back to regroup. The movement was barely visible through the foliage but they could tell it was friendlies. Like yesterday's files of returning walking wounded, the sight was not a morale booster.

Most of those who fell back waited for others to join them, wisely not wanting to move again in anything less than squad-strength. One group of four or five men, however, set off boldly back up the hill, right in front of 3rd Squad's line of march.

There were now RPG's coming in with the small arms fire.

Everyone in 3rd Squad was watching the smaller group of four or five move up when a Claymore mine, placed somewhere in a tree, exploded with a flat bang. Each member of the unknown group was thrown to his chest, peppered with a lethal fuselade of miniature ball bearings. Their backs were sheets of blood.

With the detonation of the Claymore, 3rd Squad itself began taking small arms fire. Terry Frantz had at first assumed that one of the unlucky group ahead had tripped a wire to detonate the Claymore but now realized it had been command-detonated by the same NVA unit that was now trying to pin 3rd Squad. If it hadn't been for the unknown troops in front, it would have been 3rd Squad under the Claymore. Back in basic training, they had demonstrated the curved wedge-shaped Claymore's killing power by having one shatter a wall of two-by-fours from a distance of five feet.

Once again, Terry Frantz had no time to think about what might have been. It didn't matter who the unlucky bastards ahead had been. All that mattered was getting his own men out—*now*. He and Murphy had taken cover behind a pair of splintered tree trunks and were trying to focus on their map without raising their heads.

"Cold Steel. Cold Steel," cried Murphy into the radio, trying to make contact and bring in artillery or gunships. "This is One Six Alpha, over." He cut himself off as an RPG round whistled over his head.

Before the rocket-propelled grenade detonated, Douglas Worcester had dived from nowhere into Frantz and Murphy's position. He snapped his instructions to the RTO without waiting for a greeting or a situation report. "Tell Six Actual that the little bastards have Claymores in the trees and are blowing the shit out of us!" he cried. "Then get us some goddam fire support!"

Terry Frantz looked on in awe as well as relief.

Murphy responded to the intruder's demands immediately but could raise no one on the radio. All frequencies were filled with angry, static-filled voices making the same plea he wanted to make himself. He shrugged helplessly to Worcester and Frantz. They showed no sympathy; he looked away from them and kept trying to get through.

Worcester reached calmly to Frantz's steel pot and pulled out the pack of Lucky Strike cigarettes stuck into the elastic band. There were four cigarettes in the package, which resembled the boxes that candy cigarettes were sold in back in the World. He offered Frantz one and looked longingly up the hill to the hidden bunker line from where he was certain the Claymore had been detonated.

Worcester was certain it was a bunker line because of the even field of fire. There had not been a single muzzle flash from the flanks. They *had* to be dug back in bunkers, to stall *all* of Bravo Company like this.

"We can't get our dead and wounded out until we suppress the fire from that bunker line," he told Frantz solemnly.

"No shit," mumbled Terry Frantz.

As they were speaking, Murphy got his radio contact and started calling in the fire mission. In the background, to the right, where Worcester had crawled from to join Frantz and Murphy, Lieutenant Eden was calmly yelling orders to whoever would listen.

"*Move* those men," the lieutenant cried, "*out*."

It was the command voice of a leader rather than a green Officer Candidate School graduate.

Frantz took one long drag on his Lucky Strike, letting Worcester's words sink in.

Not even Worcester, let alone anyone in 3rd Squad or anywhere else in the company, yet realized that there were not just one but a total of three different bunker lines staring down at them, each one higher and better reinforced than the one before it. The first one, which 3rd Squad began approaching as soon as Terry Frantz flicked his cigarette on the ground, was fortified with teakwood logs and covered with mounds of dirt and foliage. Trenches and tunnels connected the fighting positions of each separate bunker. It was the kind of semipermanent defense most people would have associated with France in World War I or Saipan in World War II but never Vietnam in 1969.

Frantz split the squad into two fire teams: one led by himself, followed by Languilli, Murphy, and the machine-gun team of Duffy and Gaigin; the other led by Motown, followed by Washburn, Bienstock, and Beletsky. As the two lines moved past the blood-soaked bodies where the Claymore had gone off, the bunker nearest them came alive with a shower of small arms fire. Fortunately, however, the fire wasn't yet zeroed in on 3rd Squad. Seeing the muzzle flashes, Frantz crouched lower and motioned for Motown to move his team slower. The bunker was less than a hundred feet away.

At the same instant, Motown spotted the glint of movement in the trench linking the two nearest bunkers. He opened fire but was immediately pinned by the enemy in the nearest bunker as well as the trench. They had seen the anxious American's muzzle flash and were zeroing in.

Duffy and Gaigin, in turn, reacted instantly and instinctively, laying down support from the M60 to divert the enemy fire from Motown.

At the same time, Frantz and Languilli began tossing the fragmentation grenades toward the trench. Persuaded that the enemy was confused as to which area to concentrate on, Frantz led Languilli and Murphy forward in a low crawl. Duffy and Gaigin were still laying down covering fire for Motown.

To Frantz's own surprise, they were able to get within sixty feet of the very edge of the first bunker without apparently being detected. Before he could plot his next move, however, two long-handled Chicom grenades floated down from the bunker in a high-angled arc.

The grenades exploded to the rear of the three Americans, not hurting any of them.

Though not hit by any shrapnel, however, all three of the crawling men were momentarily stunned by the concussion; long enough for a team of NVA soldiers to rise boldly, in plain view, at the edge of the trench. They fired again in Motown's direction.

Realizing that Frantz was stunned but also that Motown was nearly nailed, Duffy pushed himself to his feet and charged up the hill toward the bunker and trench line with his big M60 tucked against his side and blazing in one continuous burst.

Duffy made it all the way to the trench line. Spotting the three NVA who were firing from the trench toward Motown, he opened up with one short burst, as Gaigin and the drill instructors would have wanted him to. He nailed all three before they realized he was there. Motown was now free to maneuver his ass.

Gaigin had nearly reached Duffy's side when he tripped over the shoulders of another NVA emerging from a spider hole. He hadn't even seen either the guy or the camouflaged hole, which was really an entrance and exit to the tunnels that served as auxiliary links between all the bunkers. The NVA scrambled out after Gaigin and began wrestling with him.

"Duffy!" cried Gaigin. "Duffy!"

Duffy turned immediately to his friend's voice. He rushed to the two wrestlers and waited until the NVA was rolled over on his back before putting the hot barrel of the pig against his temple and firing a single shot.

Gaigin saw another NVA behind Duffy aiming at him. He yelled "Watch out!" as he fired. The American machine gunner was still watching the contortion and expansion in the opposite side of the man's head where the bullet exited when he himself caught one in the arm. The bullet tore through flesh and muscle and sent him sprawling on top of Gaigin.

Rolling over and looking up, with Duffy still on top of him, Gaigin then saw another NVA approaching from less than five yards away. The man was looking directly at him and lifting his rifle to fire but then, like his buddy, caught one in the side of the skull.

Gaigin had no idea who had nailed him and didn't care.

The rest of 3rd Squad was charging the bunker line just the way it was done in the movies, on line and with rifles blazing. They paused to drop grenades into every spider hole they found.

"Secure this area!" yelled Terry Frantz. With his ears still ringing from the concussion of the Chicom grenade, he did not realize how loud he was yelling. Other grenades were going off all around him, with all their shrapnel and impact funneled into the spider holes and trenches.

They had finally reached the first bunker line.

"Motown!" yelled Frantz. "Cover that right flank! Gaigin, set up that gun!"

"Duffy needs a medic!" retorted Gaigin, again rolling over, holding his friend's shoulders. "Where's Doc?"

Frantz then turned to Murphy. "Get Worcester on the horn," he commanded, "and tell him we *got* his goddam bunker! Get Worcester on the horn."

"Say again!" yelled Murphy as grenades continued exploding and small arms erupted farther along the trench. "I can't hear you!"

Murphy was left speechless and paralyzed when Beletsky, the whimperer and worrier, grabbed the handset from him. "One Six Charlie," Beletsky called into the radio, calmly. "This is One Six Alpha, over. Be advised that bunker line is taken and secured. Send medic.'' He then paused to glance at Duffy, who was conscious and gritting his teeth silently. ''Nonpriority,'' Beletsky added. Looking around at the rest of the squad, who were staring at him with their mouths half-open in disbelief, he could think of nothing more to add. ''Over,'' he snapped, and then returned the handset to Murphy.

''Say again your last,'' came back Worcester.

As Beletsky repeated his request for medical assistance, the rest of 3rd Squad fanned out along the fighting trench between the two bunkers they had just taken. Enemy soldiers lay along the trench in the same positions and poses as when they had died. There was still intermittent sniper fire and *whooshing* RPG fire from farther up the hill but their own position was at last secure—for the moment.

Lieutenant Eden and Worcester's element soon joined them. Rather than take a break or tell war stories, however, everyone methodically went about his business preparing for whatever might come next.

Lieutenant Eden began talking on the radio and addressing Worcester at the same time, jamming his finger at the tight group of concentric ovals on his map and then pointing up the hill. He informed his superiors that the bunker line was taken and was in turn reprimanded for falling behind the plan of advance.

Washburn began handing out new bandoliers of ammo that had been brought up by the lieutenant's element.

Motown broke open a wooden box of grenades, splitting the boards apart with the grooved barrel of his M16. He carefully removed each one from its cylindrical casing before passing it up the line.

Gaigin, at Frantz's side, watched intently as Doc changed the bandage on his buddy Duffy's wound. The original bandage was already soaked through but Duffy, thanks to one of Doc's magic morphine injections, felt no pain.

The body of the NVA soldier who Gaigin had watched buy the farm with a shot that seemed to come from nowhere lay ten yards away.

"Sarge." Gaigin tapped Terry Frantz as he looked at the sprawled body. "I asked everybody, 'Who got the dink that was on me and Numbnuts,' and nobody did it. Did you?"

"Maybe he died of natural causes."

"Half his head is blown away."

"That sounds like a natural cause to me," said Doc, with a knowing wink.

"When can you get him out?" asked Frantz, referring to Duffy.

Doc nodded up the hill. "There are beaucoup fucked-up dudes from Third Platoon ahead of Duffy."

"Don't mean nothing," said Duffy himself, watching the black medic's efficient hands. "Where's my weapon?"

Duffy and everyone else ducked reflexively as a trio of V-winged F-4 Phantom jet fighters shrieked over the unseen crest of the hill. They were dropping napalm canisters, to defoliate the hill and flush out any of the enemy that might be dumb enough not to be hiding in the tunnels and covered bunkers.

The canisters made no sound on impact but immediately ignited with a loud *whoosh*, like gasoline poured on hot coals. The jets were quickly joined by two hog helicopter gunships.

Blackjack had called on his colleagues back at base camp for their high-technology support. They were obliging proudly, as if they didn't realize that the enemy had been through this ritual hundreds more times than they had. The enemy would not reemerge until the technology was called off.

The helicopter gunships were the same basic Hueys used to transport the grunts in combat assaults but had been fitted with rocket pods and Vulcan cannons. They also had sealed side doors. The Vulcan cannons, mini-guns as the troops called them, were controlled from the cockpit. They looked like scaled-down versions of the old cowboy Gatling gun but fired six hundred rounds a minute in a steady noise that sounded like a constant charge of electricity rather than anything remotely resembling a traditional machine gun. The long rockets carried both high-explosive and flechette warheads. The high explosive was to penetrate fortifications. The flechettes, which were literally short nails with fins where the flat head of a normal nail would have been, were for personnel. Each warhead held thousands of flechettes. They would fan out after the rocket had traveled and spun far enough to detonate the warhead.

Under the aerial cover, other squads of infantry began to start up the hill on both sides of 3rd Squad's triumphant position in the fighting trench.

"Let's *move,* people," barked Terry Frantz, taking the cue, "and take this fucking hill!"

As 3rd Squad began moving up through the splintered trees and crisscrossing trenches, other soldiers moved up faster on the flanks. Artillery was joining the Phantoms and hog gunships in the show.

A few NVA were breaking from their cover, charging frantically up the hill in the face of the approaching U.S. infantry. Smiles replaced the grimaces that had gripped the GIs' faces just five minutes earlier. They could at last feel the victory within their grasp.

Duffy fired at the retreating NVA and rushed forward into the trench line, yelling, ''Ammo, Gaigs. Give me some ammo!''

The sense of impending victory was shattered instantly, however, as the macho fly-boys in the helicopters got too carried away with their sense of power. Terry Frantz watched helplessly as a squad of Americans entered the second tier of bunkers and trenches only to be strafed by the hogs' electric mini-guns. Almost immediately, the American artillery was redirected to bracket the GIs who had taken the enemy's positions.

''No,'' Frantz mumbled as the grunts ahead threw down their weapons and waved their arms at the helicopters, only to be cut down and even severed at the waist by the six-hundred-round-per-minute Vulcan cannons and shrieking flechette rockets. ''No.''

Murphy yelled into his radio handset louder and more frantically than ever. ''Cease fire!'' he screamed. ''Cease fire, goddammit! You're killing our people!''

Frantz could not believe the instant carnage. The NVA who had just seconds ago been forced to flee farther up the hill were now running back to their original positions as the helicopters continued to focus on the Americans. The NVA were soon back in the second tier of bunkers, with the Phantoms and their napalm long gone. The enemy were laying down a heavy field of fire at 3rd Squad, all of who scrambled back into the bottom tier of trenches and bunkers.

Around Terry Frantz and his men, other elements who had passed 3rd Squad and come so close to taking the hill were now scampering over the first tier of trenches. They were headed back to the base of the hill, dragging their dead and wounded at their heels.

Gaigin crawled forward and looked into the smoldering bunker where Duffy had disappeared. He looked for what seemed a very long time before turning away and leaning against a charred tree trunk. Frantz saw and recognized the tragic intensity of his grief. The most feared, cruelest moment had overtaken Gaigin with the accidental death of his closest and only friend.

Chapter Thirteen

Terry Frantz and the rest of 3rd Squad, 1st Platoon, went about stoically setting up their night positions in the same enemy trenches and bunkers that had turned out to be the farthest point of advance rather than the staging point for what should have been the final triumphant assault on the crest of the hill. They all knew the Phantom and hog crews would be back at Camp Evans or Phu Bai eating hot chow and drinking cold beer that night while all of Bravo Company tried as best it could to ignore the smell of blood and the groans of the numb wounded coming from the medical evacuation area at the base of the hill. But they all knew that was the way it was. Period.

There it is. It don't mean nothing.

The quiet gloom that pervaded 3rd Squad's sector of the perimeter was reinforced when it began drizzling again just before dusk. The entire area, so heavily denuded and cratered by today's fighting, was quickly transformed into a sea of mud. The trench network was more like an irrigation ditch network. Everyone knew they would remain soaked to the bone all night.

Despite the latest bad hand dealt by chance and destiny, however, the troops tried as best they could to relax and think of more pleasant circumstances in the final moments before darkness.

Terry Frantz proceeded to make another batch of C-ration stew in his steel pot. This time, all of the FNGs contributed a meal and shared in the banquet.

Bienstock called off the names from the olive drab cans as each new item was added: "Franks and beans, beenies and weenies, spaghetti and bull's balls, ham and mother-fuckers . . ."

" 'Loosiana' hot sauce cuts through it all," said Frantz as he stirred it with a bayonet that had been sanitized by dipping the blade in a mud pool and then wiping it dry with someone's borrowed black Screaming Eagle neckerchief.

"I'm not eating that shit," declared Beletsky.

Languilli, at Worrier's side, was again poring over his prized automobile brochures. "It is *definitely* the 'Vette," he announced, oblivious to the debate he had interrupted.

"You can't score in a 'Vette," Beletsky told him.

"Will you stop finger fucking his dream with your chickenshit details," said Murphy. "Let me tell you something, Lingoolie, I have boom-boomed at Mama-san's, at a garbage dump, and under a deuce-and-a-half while girl-san read *Life* magazine and drank a Pepsi. You can score in a 'Vette. After this shit, you owe it to yourself."

As usual, the respite was soon shattered. This time it was the arrival of Platoon Sergeant Worcester, rather than the enemy, that brought them back to the reality of their plight. Worcester was approaching with two brand-new FNGs in tow.

No one in 3rd Squad had expected any replacements. Especially the four surviving FNGs who had arrived just a few days ago but already subconsciously considered themselves seasoned veterans after all they had witnessed and endured at the village and on this supposedly near-deserted hill. Everyone stared blankly, helplessly, at the two men's innocent clean-shaven faces. The faces and clean clothes only served to remind everyone in 3rd Squad of how many lifetimes ago it had been since they too had reported for duty with Bravo Company.

The two men's stitched names, DARITY and CUMMINGS, glared boldly from the stiff new patches sewn above the right breast pocket. Their weapons, as well as their fatigues, rucksacks, and camouflage helmet covers, were brand spanking new. The only things muddy were their boots. They shifted their weight uneasily from one foot to the other but dared not try to shift the weight of the flesh-cutting rucksacks as the filthy veterans eyeballed them. They knew they didn't belong here but also knew from the others' pitiful gaze that none of them did, either.

The veterans avoided small talk with the two replacements and answered the few questions they were bold enough to ask with the same cold disdain shown all FNGs. The two assumed their assigned places in the perimeter, at the edge of the fighting trench, without comment, trying to hold back the tears and whimpers they wanted to release. Having been flown out in a medevac bird, they had already seen more blood and corpses than most soldiers would during their entire tour of duty.

Each man in Bravo Company was ordered to stay on alert until midnight, regardless of his designated shift for guard or radio watch. Men lay soaked and shivering in the mud all along the lowest ring of the hill, peering out nervously at the menacing shadows and foliage before them.

Despite the alert, one man would try to duck down for a nap as his buddy kept watch. Others would reapply the stinking mosquito repellant from olive drab plastic squeeze bottles while others smoked beneath the ponchos that were proving near useless against the drizzle and mud. One troop smoked through cupped hands, unaware of the light seeping out through the flesh of his fingers, but no one chastised him. Other men along the line were whispering into their radios' black plastic handsets.

"Commo check," one radio would whisper statically to another.

"Lazy crazy, Ho Chi Minh" came back Murphy's reply for 3rd Squad to each call.

"Same-same," would respond the anonymous caller. "Thank you much."

Third Squad, 1st Platoon, indulged in none of the others' slacking off. No one slept or smoked in the section of mud trenches that was their sector of 1st Platoon's perimeter. It was as if the kidding over Frantz's C-ration stew and Languilli's Corvette had never occurred. Bienstock, Beletsky, and Languilli stared intently into the darkness. The FNG Cummings mimicked them, close to Bienstock's side. Terry Frantz's eyes darted back and forth from one shadow to another.

Frantz kept moving his eyes to prevent any one object from blurring or distorting any other motion in the darkness: protecting your night vision, they called it back at Fort Campbell.

As the night wore on, however—with his boots weighing a ton apiece in the water and mud, with the mosquitoes growing more ferocious and his body sweating and shivering at the same time—he made the classic FNG mistake of letting himself think he saw movement in a charred formation of trees and then staring directly at it. Before he knew it, the bare trees were waddling sideways and then marching toward him like a Jules Verne monster. He finally blinked and shook his head to snap himself out of it. He then wiped his brow and checked his men before commencing again to scan the terrain before him.

Not even Frantz's methodical and professional scanning could detect the movement actually taking place just a few meters above the charred tree formation, however. The NVA regulars who had fled the Phantoms' napalm less than twelve hours ago were regrouped and stalking their enemy with a coolness, patience, and determination that made Bravo Company's current status look like a child's party.

The NVA riflemen breathed slowly and evenly as they inched forward. Their equipment made only the faintest noise as it jostled against their bodies, inaudible to the GIs. They nodded to each other upon seeing the first red glow of a cigarette, making mental notes of the exact location.

Behind the riflemen came the sappers, identical in size as well as dress to Han, the *chieu hoi* demonstrator. Each sapper wore only shorts and had greased his face and body black. Each carried nothing but a few grenades, rubber bands, and the satchel charges he would drop into the unsuspecting enemy's positions.

The commanding officer, whose uniform had no insignia of rank, wore a soft cap rather than the daytime pith helmet. He had camouflaged his face, like the sappers, and used hand signals to maneuver his elements into place and send them on their missions. Unlike the miserable sweating GIs, his face revealed no sweat or any other sign of fear or fatigue.

He moved a heavy machine gun team into the tree line and then sent his riflemen and RPG grenadiers down the hill behind the slinking sappers. The riflemen stopped and lay prone a hundred meters above the edge of 3rd Squad's perimeter. The sappers then dropped to their knees to begin crawling the rest of the way to their objective.

The greased sappers snaked forward swiftly and silently through the mud, feeling gingerly in a wide radius with their fingers before pulling their weight forward. One of them stopped before a Claymore mine that had been placed just ten feet from the berne of the trench line. After feeling around it for trip wires, he calmly lifted it by the base of the tripod spikes, holding it upright in the mud, and turned it 180 degrees, so that it would explode back at the GIs when detonated.

Another sapper, ten feet left of this one, found a trip wire in one of his finger sweeps. He followed it delicately, with thumb and forefinger, to the trip flare where it ended. He then put a rubber band around the flare's detonator and cut the wire, eliminating the menace.

A third sapper had reached the point where all of his comrades had pinpointed the rosy burning cigarette glare. The GI was still smoking and the man at his side had dozed off. The sapper eased over the edge of the trench and cupped one hand over the smoker's mouth as he slit his throat with a commandeered stiletto held in the other. Easing all the way into the trench, still not making a sound, he repeated the smooth *coup de grace* with the sleeping troop, catching the helmet from the slumping body to prevent it from making any noise.

Other sappers crawled right past the men on guard and entered the defensive perimeter without being detected. Moving toward the center of the perimeter and the GIs' PRC-25 radios, they began dropping their delayed-fuse satchel charges near 1st Platoon's fighting positions.

Douglas Worcester was sipping a cup of coffee at the center of the perimeter. He squatted, Vietnamese-style, beside Lieutenant Eden, Murphy, and the radio. He was unconsciously massaging his scalp with his right hand as the three discussed the GIs' most sacred topic, how to score with American girls back in the World.

"Most girls won't even talk to a guy if they think he's in the army," Worcester was saying. "You have to have hair to get laid. Why else would I be cultivating on my head what naturally grows on my ass?" He paused ever so briefly, sniffing the air. His facial muscles and shoulders immediately tightened. He silently mouthed the word *gooks* and reached for an illumination flare before calmly resuming his lecture.

"These kids call me 'Old Man,' " he said, with the flare at his side, positioned to pop. "They must think I have rust on my pecker."

He slapped the rear end of the flare against his knee to send it *whoosh*ing up into the night sky and in the same instant scrambled for his fighting gear. The flare erupted a hundred feet overhead in a shower of green sparks, like Fourth of July fireworks.

It was the signal that the perimeter had been infiltrated: a signal with which the North Vietnamese Army was just as familiar as were the GIs themselves. The sappers leaped to their feet and began dropping grenades and satchel charges randomly into the nearest fighting positions as they ran through the area.

The stunned men of 1st Platoon began firing into their own perimeter, just as the NVA commander would have wanted them to. The odds of shooting one of their own with the automatic and semiautomatic fire were far greater than the odds of shooting one of the zigzagging sappers.

Worcester screamed into the radio, "All units, stop firing into the perimeter! I say again, goddammit, stop firing into the perimeter!"

Spotting one of the greased sappers himself, he picked up an entrenching tool and started chasing him. It was like a little boy chasing a greased piglet, with Worcester zigzagging through the perimeter holding the collapsible shovel high above his own head, oblivious to the firing that still hadn't completely died out from his own troops' positions.

Someone else on another radio had called for illumination flares. The entire perimeter glowed yellow under the drifting parachute-tailed balls of fire.

The Americans in the trenches and bunkers had also finally begun to get their act together and were returning the fire coming at them from above. Each man still kept glancing over his shoulder for sappers as he fired.

As soon as the NVA commander signaled for his machine gun to open up, the Vietnamese regulars charged down the hill with AK-47 rifles blazing. The grenadiers would occasionally stop and fall to one knee to fire a rocket-propelled grenade, but the covering fire of the machine gun and riflemen kept the Americans from nailing them.

Frantz and Motown began throwing grenades themselves, ignoring the machine-gun bullets tearing into the ground before them. The whizzing and thudding bullets sent dirt flying into their eyes. Satchel charges were still going off around them.

They could hear no screams or groans of the wounded above the sharp deafening noise of the battle. The nauseating smell of cordite gunpowder filled the sickly yellow area.

Cummings, the FNG, was firing on full automatic between Frantz and Bienstock. Just as he thought he saw the squad leader nod to him that he was doing a good job, he turned and saw four NVA charging directly at him. He picked up the Claymore detonator that Bienstock had stuck into the mud, just inside the edge of the trench, and waited for them to get even closer.

"No!" cried Frantz, but it was already too late. The FNG had either not heard the warning or been too carried away with his own adrenaline to pay attention.

Bienstock ducked but had no time to drag the replacement down with him. The Claymore's tiny ball bearing missiles flew across Cummings's face, decimating eyes, nose, and all other features at the close range before the FNG even had a chance to gasp, let alone scream.

The four unscathed NVA jumped right over Bienstock and the dead troop without breaking stride. Frantz jumped up and began chasing them, the way Worcester had the sapper. Unlike Worcester, however, Frantz had an M16 with a full magazine. He nailed all four in the back just as Motown yelled for everyone to duck. Frantz was amazed that the black man's voice could be heard.

"Everybody down!" yelled Motown. "Down! Blow those Claymores. *Now*!"

The Claymores blew on his command, exploding over 3rd Squad's own position as the NVA had planned when they turned them around. The clever

NVA had not planned on being in the perimeter themselves when they were blown, however.

Frantz counted three go down with their backs arched inversely but had no time to gloat. Worcester was running along the trench, trying to rally and regroup the entire platoon with no apparent concern for his own safety. "Pull back to the CP!" he called, motioning down the hill with his free arm. "Pull back, in *order,* goddammit."

Worcester saw his friend Frantz pointing his rifle directly at his face. Frantz was yelling but Worcester couldn't hear. Instinctively, Worcester hit the prone and let Frantz blow away the near-naked sapper who had been crouched five feet behind him. The sapper had held a grenade.

No one bothered to pick the grenade up as 3rd Squad finally began withdrawing toward the base of the hill where they had set up the medical evacuation area yesterday afternoon, when they had still hoped they would be leaving the hill for a hot meal in a few hours.

Just ahead, Terry Frantz was reloading his weapon. At Frantz's side, Murphy was calling in an artillery barrage on the PRC-25. Glancing up from his map, Murphy saw another NVA approaching in a run. The RTO calmly drew the .45 automatic from his canvas pistol belt and killed him with one shot in the chest, then continued talking on the radio without missing a beat.

"Fire mission!" Murphy cried. "Twelve gooks in the open, grid 0163-7862. Willie Peter. Up two hundred . . ."

Terry Frantz had stopped firing, running out of targets at last, and was scanning the charred tree line. The sky was still yellow with the lingering parachute illumination flares. Suddenly, he heard the screams and all the groans of the wounded. It was a sound he had heard countless times before but was more terrifying each time. Somewhere to his right he heard an indignant voice that sounded like Doc's but could have come from anyone on Hill 937.

"This hill is making hamburger out of all of us!" cried the anonymous voice.

No one anywhere on Hill 937, American or Vietnamese, realized that the anonymous cry had forever made the topographical map's cold numbers irrelevant. From that night on, in *Time* and *Newsweek* magazine stories as well as on the six o'clock television news and, much later, the history books, this place would be known as Hamburger Hill.

Chapter Fourteen

Survivors kept straggling down the hill to the medical evacuation area all night and into the mist-veiled morning. The uniforms were tattered and, as often as not, blood-spattered. The faces were drained of all emotion. All of them gazed ahead with Open Grave eyes, carrying nothing more than their weapons. The rucksacks and all other equipment save a few magazines or bandoliers of ammunition had been jettisoned before the retreat.

Each man was greeted at the edge of the littered area by the burned hulk of a medevac helicopter that had taken a B-40 rocket at some point during the night-long battle. Immediately beyond the destroyed helicopter—a fifteen-million-dollar piece of the most advanced hardware in the Americans' arsenal, downed by a World War II–design grenade worth maybe fifty dollars on the open market—each new arrival was confronted by a circle of fifteen to twenty severely wounded, lying in the mud awaiting another bird. These men were being ministered by the few medics who had made it down and by less severely wounded volunteer assistants while everyone else either pulled guard or tried to rest while awaiting whatever Blackjack had lined up for morning. The most severely wounded begged for food and water but the medics had given their ad hoc assistants strict orders not to give in to the pleas. They didn't need stomach convulsions on top of everything else.

Third Squad, 1st Platoon, huddled among the less severely wounded, sharing whatever C-ration food and water they managed to scrounge from the supplies that littered the ground. The supplies had been dumped by helicopter crews too anxious to get out to let their skids any closer than within five feet of the ground.

A chaplain knelt by a man with a bandaged face. No one knew when the chaplain had arrived—with a medevac bird the previous evening, Frantz assumed. The fair-skinned, clean-uniformed officer was leaning close to the troop's heavily bandaged mouth, trying futilely to understand what the man was saying. The troop's layered bandages were crusty with dried blood but he was fully conscious.

Sensing the chaplain's uneasiness, Terry Frantz nudged him and handed him his own canteen and his last two cans of fruit. Frantz knew that was what the wounded man wanted. The first thing any conscious wounded man always asked for was either a cigarette or a can of fruit.

"Don't worry, chaplain," he said, "grunts never die—"

"You just smell that way," interrupted the chaplain to finish the joke.

"How come you have a weapon, padre?" demanded Beletsky, gazing at the .45 automatic at the officer's waist.

"God made me a priest, not a fool."

"I'll buy that," said Beletsky, summing up the entire squad's approval.

*   *   *

Within five minutes of that remark, Bienstock and the rest of 3rd Squad were on the move again, filing past a neat line of muddy boots and ankles extending from the ponchos that covered the rest of their owners' dead bodies. They were on their way to their newly assigned command post, along with all the rest of 1st Platoon, at the base of the hill but farther to the flank of the medevac area. When told that this would be where they would dig in for now, they ignored standard procedure and proceeded immediately to erect makeshift clotheslines out of vines and bamboo, to hang their socks out to dry.

Lieutenant Eden was barking into the radio, trying to arrange another supply drop. Like the four surviving FNGs who had set out with him, the lieutenant was no longer green. As thoroughly filthy and tattered as any other man in the platoon, he was hoarse from shouting all night to his own men and into the radio for artillery and air support. Only seventeen men were left in his platoon, which would have had forty-five men at full strength. He heard a voice over the radio: "Red One Six Alpha, Six Alpha, will try to resupply at a later time, out."

"They're going to try to supply later today," Murphy told him.

"You get Six back on the horn," ordered the lieutenant in a voice so raspy it hurt even the listener, "and tell him my men need food and water *now,* not later." He then turned to Worcester. "Give me your map," he ordered the platoon sergeant, who sat leisurely on the muddy ground.

Worcester ignored the officer.

"Let's take a look at that map, Sergeant."

"We're in the Ashau Valley, Lieutenant," replied Worcester defiantly, "and we ain't going nowhere except back up that goddam Hamburger Hill."

The lieutenant glared briefly at the man who had dragged him from the combat assault bird's skids by his ruck straps. Then, with everything that had happened since that incident flashing through his mind, he collapsed on the ground at the maddeningly wise N.C.O.'s side with no further comment.

"I'll get you a map, sir," said Worcester, in a tone that was soft and sympathetic.

The lieutenant motioned for Worcester to remain seated and lit a cigarette. Handing the smoke to his rock-steady platoon sergeant, it suddenly dawned on the college-educated officer that Worcester was probably younger than him, even though his face and actions showed decades more experience, suffering, and wisdom.

A few meters away, Gaigin, who had quietly inherited the principal gunner's job, sat fondling and cleaning his weapon. The M60 lay across his lap, looking too heavy for him to even pick up, let alone hump through the bush.

All the other troops of 3rd Squad were lounging lazily, the way they would have back in the security of base camp. The bloods Motown, Doc, and Washburn sat together jiving in low voices. Bienstock, sporting a grenade pin that he had twisted into a peace symbol on the same neck chain where his mezuzah hung, sat off to himself reading a letter. Beletsky, ever conscious of taking all precautions and following all advice, was sprinkling foot powder onto his ankles and feet. Frantz and Beletsky's hooch-mate Languilli were taking turns with Frantz's razor, scraping the stubble from their faces without the benefit of soap or mirror.

"Hey, Sarge," called Beletsky, "do you think they'll send up more foot powder in the supply?"

Frantz yelled at him with no inhibition. "Will you stop worrying about nothing, for Christ's sake? So you have bad feet when you get back to the World, what the hell can they do to you, send you to Vietnam?"

"My skin's peeling off!" continued Beletsky, raising his foot for all to see. "I've gone from an eleven D to a ten C. I'm a *salesman,* my feet are my life."

Bienstock was the only man who didn't glance reflexively at Beletsky's sickly white and shriveled foot. Bienstock was staring through his letter into the bowels of the earth.

"It's from my girlfriend," he finally announced. "She says she's not going to write me anymore."

Finally glancing over to the lonely Queens native, Languilli was sorry for his friend. The grief and shock on Bienstock's face were worse than that of any of the other men who had witnessed and smelled so much death in the past forty-eight hours. The grief and shock on Bienstock's face were the GI's ultimate nightmare: the DJ, Dear John letter, from the girl back home. The girl back home was the fantasy that made those nights with a cold wet air mattress and the company of kamikaze ants and chirping lizards bearable. The girl back home made it possible to tell yourself that *you* wouldn't end up limbless or dead.

Bienstock ignored him and kept staring at the pastel paper. "Her friends at college told her that it was 'immoral,' " he said with his chin quivering, "to write to me."

No one, not even worldly Vincent Languilli, knew how to react. The GIs' most practiced cynicism failed at such moments, when their true position among their peers back in the World was brought home with the impact of an eight-inch artillery round. Normally, someone would have replied immediately, "There it is," or "It don't mean nothing." But not now. Not with a DJ letter inspired by college-student morality.

Vincent Languilli rose and walked to where Bienstock sat. Without saying anything, Languilli sat down beside the jilted soldier and put his arm around his shoulder. They gazed off together at the still-virgin tree line beyond the medevac area, oblivious to the carnage and garbage surrounding them and everyone else.

As usual, the interlude for fruit eating, cigarette smoking, letter reading, and foot powdering was gone before anyone had finished whichever of the four leisure rituals he had chosen. The men of 1st Platoon were called together for new rations, ammunition, and medical supplies from the very next supply bird. They were then regrouped for another assault on the hill.

They were not informed, however, that this time the entire battalion—four rifle companies, sixteen platoons, sixty-four squads—was moving up en masse. All they were given was the specific angle they were to climb.

That angle turned out to cross a steep and slippery rock formation. Heart-stricken Bienstock ascended behind Motown, Washburn, and Gaigin. Bienstock had been made Gaigin's assistant gunner without any formal orders being issued.

Skinny Gaigin, balancing the M60 on his shoulder, had no trouble stepping up one rock to the next but heart-stricken Bienstock quickly slipped. He slid ten feet and landed on his shoulder, atop a wider slab of rock. His face contorted in a silent scream as he struggled not to let the noise escape. There was sporadic faint firing from both ahead and behind, and he did not want to be the one to broadcast their position to possible snipers or ambush teams.

Doc scrambled down to Bienstock's side like a mountain goat, panting rhythmically, medical bags flapping from his hips. The medic calmly felt the shoulder and, without warning, pulled sharply. He elicited another silent scream from his patient as he popped the joint back in place.

Doc then scampered back up the rocks without saying a word.

Bienstock fell in behind. The girl back home was finally forgotten. All that mattered now to Bienstock was keeping up with the others, holding up his own end. He was determined to do it with no winces of pain and no whimpering over what he had left behind in the World.

Fortunately, the rock climb lasted just a hundred meters. The fourteen remaining members of 1st Platoon then walked through a shallow creek, splashing toward a gentler rock formation that appeared to be near the very crest of the hill.

Lieutenant Eden was walking abreast of Murphy, ready to get on the horn to Higher as soon as they encountered anything or anyone. Worcester walked behind the lieutenant and motioned for the men behind to spread farther apart. Frantz was at point, followed by Languilli and Beletsky. As the creek narrowed they stepped out of the water, leading the others toward a small knoll.

Terry Frantz was known as the best point man in all of Bravo Company but not even he noticed the bunker dug into the rocks and grass near the creek, just before the knoll. The entrance was a tunnel and there was only the faintest slit for the enemy to see through. A rock ledge extended over the slit.

No one would have detected it, except perhaps a water snake or an NVA regular.

"Grenade!" yelled Languilli as he watched a long-handled Chicom grenade roll toward them.

The entire file hit the prone, throwing themselves on the pebbled creek bank and scampering for cover. As soon as the first grenade exploded, behind Frantz, Languilli, and Beletsky, two more rolled toward them. No one could yet tell where they were coming from.

"Where are they?" yelled Beletsky. "Where the hell are they? Do you *see* them?"

"Negative," replied Terry Frantz calmly. The squad leader cursed himself for walking into whatever it was they were about to confront. At the same time, however, he kept scanning the knoll coolly.

When the inevitable small arms fire opened up from the knoll, Vincent Languilli found himself unable to raise his head from the soft dirt. His eyes froze on a centipede crawling into the lush grass. He felt no pain or even fear. He was not even trembling, simply frozen to the ground. There was a thousand pounds pressing against his neck.

It must be like this when you're in a car wreck, he thought to himself as he tried unsuccessfully to move his neck muscles. When you're paralyzed.

The AK-47 rounds were literally zipping over his head, just like they did in old Cowboy-and-Indian movies.

Suddenly, another Chicom grenade appeared from nowhere and stopped rolling five feet in front of him. The weight suddenly evaporated. Languilli thrust himself forward like a football player breaking from the line of scrimmage. On his knees, he grabbed the grenade by the handle to toss it back where it had come from.

Without even knowing why, however, he paused to glance over his back. An NVA was taking careful aim with an AK-47, no more than ten yards away.

Languilli backhanded the grenade toward the NVA and threw himself on top of Frantz and Beletsky, who were firing randomly at faint muzzle flashes. He landed across their backs just as the grenade exploded in the air, killing the NVA but sending the rest of its shrapnel whizzing harmlessly above the Americans.

"I saw him," panted Languilli. "I *saw* him." It was the first kill Languilli could positively claim for himself. It was an exhilirating feeling. Swinging Vinnie Languilli had nailed the bastard and saved his buddies' lives.

In a more routine firefight, an ambush or a raid against a force equally or less armed than 1st Platoon, Languilli's spontaneous bravery would have brought daps and pats on the back from everyone. He would have been put in for a Bronze Star with V Device, for valor, at the very least.

On Hamburger Hill, however, there was no time to even fully comprehend such acts of valor, let alone glorify them. As soon as one deed was done, everyone was regrouping for yet another phase of the endless circular ritual. Ruck up or dig in, move up or fall back, call in medevacs or call in Phantoms or hogs.

By now, the pattern of fighting had become so routine and ritualistic and the men of 1st Platoon had become so thoroughly exhausted that nothing could surprise them. Their actions and reactions were methodical and instinctive, motivated by raw adrenaline itself rather than conscious fear or determination. No one bothered to congratulate Languilli when the firefight ended, nor did Languilli expect them to.

Chapter Fifteen

Vietnam wasn't supposed to be what 1st Platoon, Bravo Company, was now encountering. It was supposed to be small units against small units. Contact was supposed to be furious but short. Mr. Nathaniel Victor *never* chose to wage a protracted battle over any piece of ground, let alone a hill in the middle of the jungle whose only significance happened to be that it was in both armies' line of march. Mr. Nathaniel Victor always saved his firepower and his manpower for those surprise actions like village raids and fire base sapper attacks, to deprive the Screaming Eagles of the 101st Airborne Division the satisfaction of being able to confront him head-on the way it had been done in Europe nearly thirty years ago. Mr. Nathaniel Victor always smirked and laughed as he faded back into the jungle.

Until now. Now he was taking the Screaming Eagles head-on, the way the old brown-shoe army officers like Blackjack had been praying he would. Blackjack and the generals back at base camp and the politicians back in the World were finally being given the chance to prove what they had boasted ever since entering the quagmire of Vietnam, that their troops were man-for-man the best fighters in the world. With the Americans' leader Richard

Nixon talking about Vietnamization, turning the bulk of the fighting over to the ARVN, Army of the Republic of Vietnam, Mr. Nathaniel Victor had apparently decided to put the boast to the test. He knew that if the Screaming Eagles folded against him, the well equipped but less motivated ARVN would run like dogs.

None of the weary men of Bravo Company put their plight or their mission in such geopolitical terms, however. They thought in terms of the different phases of the ritual.

Now, with the firing stopped and the rock-covered bunker blown asunder by C-4 *plastique,* it was time for the medevac phase. First, the tops of the hill and the knoll in front of 1st Platoon were thoroughly strafed by Huey hog gunships and napalm-bosomed Phantoms. The medevac birds came in right behind, with the Phantoms still circling high above and the helicopter gunships hovering closer. Because of the grade and the remaining trees, the medevac choppers used their jungle penetrators this time. The penetrators were winches, extended over the side of the ship by a folding metal arm, with a seat at the end of the steel cable that looked like the seat of a playground swing.

Miraculously, none of the medevac birds or their slowly rising passengers took any sniper fire. Nonetheless, the Phantoms and gunships returned to again burn and pepper the ground each time before another medevac was allowed to come in. The routine continued on into the evening, with 1st Platoon still set up beneath the creek and the knoll.

Everyone's nerves had been stretched to the limit by now, and no one tried to hide it. Lieutenant Eden, Worcester, Frantz, and the other squad leaders again huddled around a map and a circle of radios for another discussion of tactics and objectives. None of them knew any simple way to get to the top of the hill, however. All of them knew the huddle was meaningless.

Beletsky had produced a cassette tape from his hip pocket and crawled to cool Motown's position to borrow his tape player. Motown gave it to him as naturally and casually as if he had been a brother blood.

"Put the tape in there and press that button," the black rifleman explained.

A gloating Beletsky waved the tape in front of Motown's face before inserting it. "It's from my girl," he bragged. "Claire . . ."

"Just don't use all the juice," barked Motown, the naturalness and hospitality gone.

Beletsky wanted to give the damn machine back, wanted to tell him he didn't *need* any favors if that was the way he felt. Glancing again at Claire's cassette, however, he decided easily that he would rather put up with the insolence for her sake than fight him and lose the chance to hear her. He could always fight him later.

Beletsky took the tape player without saying thank you and walked toward his buddies Languilli and Bienstock.

Bienstock was digging a fighting hole for himself with his short-handled, backbreaking entrenching tool. Languilli was studying the centerfold from a *Playboy* magazine that had arrived on the same supply bird as Beletsky's tape.

"Now *that's* 'immoral, unjust, and illegal,' " declared Languilli as he held the girl up for Bienstock's approval. "I was in college six months," he continued, "and every time someone said 'Vietnam,' a thousand people would yell out 'immoral, unjust, and illegal.' "

Bienstock dug harder. Languilli had only reminded him of the letter from the girl he had managed to forget while climbing the rock formation. "We should bust their heads open," he said to his entrenching tool, referring to the college students rather than the enemy, "and pour some of Hamburger Hill into them, and then we'll see how much they know."

Languilli continued to try to get Bienstock to lighten up as Beletsky, just three feet away, assumed a Vietnamese squat position and turned on Claire's sweet voice.

"She likes to lie naked on the beach and have her boyfriend read *The Prophet* to her," said Languilli as he continued to study the centerfold.

"It's me again," Claire was saying. "I forgot where I left off, so I'll start again. I just don't know what to say."

Bienstock shoveled even more furiously and deliriously. "He's probably a long-haired Four-F faggot," he replied to Languilli.

"I don't know what time it is where you are," mused Claire, "I don't even know where you are. That's what makes it so hard."

Languilli pretended to read from the blurb beneath the smaller photos on the reverse side of the centerfold page. "I love to have him wrap his long straight hair around me while he makes love to me all night long."

Bienstock's eyes shot up incredulously. "She really said that?" he asked as Claire continued her lament.

"I try to think about you and I just can't imagine what you're doing . . ."

"She became his love prisoner," mocked Languilli. "She'll do anything for him."

". . . I had dinner with your mom and dad. We read all your letters and looked at the pictures you sent. If you can, Joe, try to smile more in the pictures, it would help your mother."

"Jesus Christ," growled Bienstock, taken in by Languilli, "I am never getting another fucking haircut."

Claire's voice grew sadder and everyone in earshot of the machine stopped talking. "Your dad didn't say much, we both know what he's like, but Catherine says he gets up early every morning and watches the news and eats his dinner in front of the TV at night. I think he's looking for you."

Her voice was getting weaker, Motown's batteries were dying. The lower tone and pace of her words only seemed to make everyone in 3rd Squad listen all the more intently, as if they had forgotten what it was like to have a girl talk to them in a voice that lacked the stress and profanity that had now become their own lives.

"I'm glad you have such good friends like Bienstock and Langerelli," she continued.

"Languilli," the proud Italian corrected her.

"And Galvan and Frantz. Joe, I want you to know one thing, *I'll* always be true to you. I'll wait for you. I know it must be very difficult for you over there and if you can't be true, if you can't wait, I'll understand. I know you love me—"

"I love this woman," Languilli again interrupted. "She's telling you to get laid."

"I wish you weren't there," mourned Claire. "I wish none of you were there. But I'm proud of you, Joe. I just don't think it's fair that everybody is back here acting like nothing is going on, their lives are the same. It's just not fair. And I don't believe what they say about you. Anyhow, I don't care, because I love all of you, especially *you*, my darling—''

Her voice died without even a click and Beletsky began shaking the machine violently.

"Take it easy with that," called Motown.

Beletsky glared at him. "I'll take it any way I can."

"I told you not to use all the batteries," said Motown, oblivious to the cause of Beletsky's anger and frustration.

"It's the goddam nigger music that you listen to," said Beletsky.

Motown pushed Beletsky, but the white man recovered quickly and tackled him. They rolled on the ground, locked together, wild with rage and struggling to get the leverage to kill each other.

Doc finally approached to break them apart. As he knelt and touched Beletsky, however, Languilli thought he was trying to intercede on Motown's behalf. Languilli jumped at Doc and the donnybrook was on, with Worcester and Frantz trying to break them all apart but ending up trading punches with all of them.

"Back off," ordered Worcester futilely. "Stop this shit," he commanded as he ducked a punch. "Beletsky—"

"Get off him," Frantz yelled to Motown. "Back off, Doc. Alphabet, put that shovel *down!*"

All eyes froze on the entrenching tool Languilli wielded above Doc's head. Languilli dropped it without any show of emotion and the fight was over, as quickly and spontaneously as it had started. Nobody had won. Nobody had lost. Nobody cared.

There it was: it didn't mean nothing.

"What's happening here?" Frantz asked Motown as everyone backed away.

Motown stared blankly into his squad leader's eyes as Beletsky handed back his cassette player. "War's happening," he informed Frantz.

Third Squad returned to the business of digging in for the night, setting Claymore mines and trip flares, and checking weapons and the radio.

There was no more action all night, either among themselves or from the enemy. The men were too tired to notice how unusual the quiet was compared to the previous two nights.

Mr. Nathaniel Victor must be as tired as we are, concluded Terry Frantz as he made the rounds to check the perimeter. He's taking a break, Frantz thought, we're *both* taking a break, the first sensible thing either one of us has done.

Ordinarily, Frantz would have given holy hell to any man he caught sleeping on guard duty. Tonight, however, he let them be. It didn't mean nothing. Even Worcester was snoring away like Archie Bunker. Frantz crawled back into his poncho hooch. Before joining everyone else in the arms of Morpheus, he prayed briefly for it to not rain again.

It didn't rain and the dawn broke clear and spectacular, with the sun itself hidden by the crest of the hill and the air smelling fresh and clean despite the enemy bodies that still lay near the stream. The men of 3rd Squad were starving but refreshed from the brief respite of a full night's merciful sleep. When Frantz announced they were pulling back to the medevac area at the base of the hill for resupply, there was an almost audible sense of relief. They moved out sprightly, as if unaware of how filthy and tattered their clothes and gear were.

The rows of men sitting and lying in line waiting for medevac birds had grown longer than ever. The pungent smell of death, of swelling and rotting organs, mixed with that of cigarette smoke and cordite. The cordite from earlier artillery and mortar barrages hung like smog over the flat denuded base of the hill. There were more hulks of burned helicopters than yesterday morning and the area itself seemed to have doubled, with twice as many people and bodies and even more than twice as many scattered and splintered ammunition crates and C-ration cartons.

Frantz picked up his pace, eager to get his men past the carnage, groans, and stench to the supply pad set up near the outer edge of the area's ad hoc defensive perimeter. He noticed a man in shiny new fatigues loitering by the sandbag helicopter pad. The man was too old and paunchy to be an FNG but there was no insignia of rank on his collar or sleeves. He didn't wear a pistol belt and had no rucksack or rifle on the ground beside him.

Finally noticing the camera hanging from the man's neck, Frantz realized it was a reporter.

The squad leader stepped out even more quickly, causing some of his men to trot to keep up. His throat was tight and he clenched his jaws. Eyeballing the shiny camera lens, all he could think of was the college boys with their long hair and deferments and the Chamber of Commerce members' sons who had dodged the draft by sneaking into the National Guard and the Reserves.

The reporter didn't notice the hateful stare but knew from the way Frantz walked that he was the leader. He did not want to talk to any leaders, however. He wanted to talk to the *common* troop. The boy from Ohio or Indiana who was grinning and bearing it for Mom and Dad and Richard Nixon, *that* was what folks wanted to see and hear. The filthier and shabbier the subject, the better.

The reporter was sorry there were no helicopters or firing in the background as he trotted around the leader without even introducing himself. "Okay, let's get this squad here," he said, then added into the mike, "Teddy Ford, Hamburger Hill, May 17th."

"How long have you been on Hamburger Hill, soldier?" he asked Bienstock.

"What day is it?" replied the stunned and puzzled grunt.

Disgusted with the unemotional response, the reporter turned to Motown. "Brother," he said with a smile, "how many times have you been up and down this hill?"

Motown stared at him defiantly. "What are you doing here?" he demanded.

"It's my job," the man replied confidently.

"Bullshit," countered Motown, standing taller and pushing his chest closer to the man's.

"We've been up and down this hill nine fucking times," interjected Doc.

Disgusted with the bad attitudes he was confronting, the reporter reluctantly turned to Frantz. Determined to get *something* to file on the next bird out, he stepped closer to him and smiled sarcastically.

"The word at Division is that you can't take this hill," he said, goading him. "What do you say about that? Even Senator Kennedy says you don't have a chance here."

Terry Frantz stepped closer to the man, whose cheeks smelled of Aqua Velva lotion. He stared right through him, causing him to pale and step back, but then spoke to him softly.

"You really like this shit, don't you?" asked Frantz.

The reporter again darted his eyes to the others, searching for sympathy, but they were all now as hostile as the leader. He was afraid for his life. He had heard about these kind of troops: ruthless animals who dropped grenades into their officers' tents; savages who cut off ears of the dead enemy as souvenirs; subhumans who could never readjust to civilian life.

"It's your job," Frantz continued. "A 'story.' You're waiting here like a fucking vulture, waiting for somebody to die so you can take a picture."

"It is my job," stammered the reporter as he backed away.

"I got more respect for those little bastards up there," declared Frantz. "At least they take a side. You just take pictures."

"Okay! Okay! You don't want me to film you, I won't," said the reporter hoarsely.

"You probably don't even do your own fucking. Un-ass my AO."

"What?"

Sensing the taut line that held Frantz back from the breaking point, Motown stepped between them. After nodding for the reporter to leave quickly, he winked at Frantz. "We got places to go, Sarge," he told him.

Ignoring Motown, Frantz continued talking to the gutless civilian's back.

"We're going to take this fucking hill, newsman!" he called to him. "And if I see you at the top taking pictures of any of my people, I will blow your fucking head off! You haven't earned the right to be here! Do you understand? Do you? *Understand?*"

He was trembling as he yelled, finally releasing at least some of the bile he had kept locked away for so long. He didn't even notice his own men circle him to hold him back and then lead him away.

Third Squad and the rest of 1st Platoon were allowed to spend the rest of the morning getting their new gear together, cleaning weapons, and resting on the ground at the edge of the medevac area. They finished the necessary chores quickly and were soon all stretched out on their backs, again thoroughly exhausted. They were oblivious to the saturation bombing under way at the top of the hill and the roaring and slapping of the medevac and supply choppers touching down and lifting off less than a hundred feet from them.

"I should have gone to Canada," mused Bienstock, again thinking of the Dear John letter and all the long-haired bums back in the World.

Languilli, at Bienstock's right, made the jacking-off gesture. "All they got is Eskimos up there," he countered.

Contemplating a life amidst the draft dodgers in Canada, Bienstock shook his head. "Fuck Canada," he said.

"The smart white people go to college," observed Doc.

Beletsky and Frantz lay on the other side of the lovelorn Bienstock, taking the conversation in with the filtered sunlight. "Not me, I'm doing my two years," said Beletsky, "getting married, and *forgetting* this shit."

"Never happen," said Frantz.

Doc continued his own train of thought as if talking to himself. "You people must be aware," he said, "that the *brothers* are here because they cannot afford an education."

"What am *I* doing," challenged Beletsky, "sitting in some fucking country club drinking Seven and Sevens and eating steak? Take a look around, Doc. I can see all kinds of white faces."

Doc finally rolled to his side and confronted the maddeningly handsome Italian. "Okay. The war started for you when you farted and said, 'Good morning, Vietnam,' " he told him, with his own pent-up frustration and bitterness again reaching the boiling point. "I was *born* into this shit."

Beletsky was unfazed, replying immediately, "And they pulled the gold fucking spoon out of my mouth so I could see how you low-class Eleven Boo's live."

Doc leaped to his feet. To the surprise of everyone except Languilli, however, the bitterness was gone from his face. He made a fist and maneuvered it down toward Beletsky in ornate circular gestures, with legs straight, bending at the waist, for the white man to dap.

"Brother *blood*," said Doc as their flesh touched. The sudden peace went unnoticed by Languilli.

"How'd you get here, Sarge?" he asked Frantz.

"Sarge, he volunteered for this shit," said Bienstock before Frantz had a chance to part his lips to speak.

"I was *drafted*, sworn in, and my hair cut before I was sober," Frantz corrected the wise guy. "The only reason I went Airborne is Collins. We volunteered for the 'reality' of it." He too shifted his body to confront Languilli. "Don't you think I chased women and good time before I got into the green machine? When we got orders for the Big Puddle, Collins says he's not going. Period. And this is one strac 'paratrooper.' He loves to jump, crawl through mud, his voice is hoarse from calling cadence, but he says, 'Fucking 'Nam is a tank.' We shipped out and this dude is still there, spit-shining his boots, smiling, saluting, and doing four miles before chow.''

"You got to respect that," commented Beletsky.

"No way," insisted Frantz. "If you don't want to pull on the little people, no sweat. Don't use your weapon. All I want from anybody is that they get their ass in the grass with the rest of us. You don't have to like it, but you have to show up."

"There it is," agreed Languilli, in an uncharacteristically serious tone.

Chapter Sixteen

That afternoon, all of Bravo Company regrouped for an assault on the opposite side of the hill. The constant bombing had apparently taken its toll, with no enemy opposition at all up to the first trench-and-bunker line, which was still filled with bloated NVA corpses.

The only opposition they encountered was the terrain itself. The bombing had been so effective that there was not a stick or blade of vegetation or other life left above the trench line. The slope between there and the distant second line of trenches and bunkers was one huge mud slide, dotted with charred and shattered tree stumps. Third Squad's clothes, faces, and weapons were dripping with globs of mud. The men's boots weighed a ton apiece as they crawled forward. Explosions at the crest and on the other side of the hill were muffled by the soft earth.

They made it easily to the second bunker line despite the mud and another rainfall. The rain was light but steady and the sky was soft dull gray. Inside the trenches, bodies of GIs were entwined with those of NVA in the frozen ballet poses of hand-to-hand combat.

Kneeling with his men inside the stinking ditch, Lieutenant Eden called out orders: "Worcester, move out Second Squad. Frantz, move your people out." He then tried to call in a report over the mud-covered radio. "Red Six, this is One Six, over," he called professionally.

There was no response. He repeated his call and slapped the black plastic handset against the back of his muddy hand. He then gave it to Murphy, who keyed it twice with the black *push-to-talk* button and immediately got the reassuring static of an open frequency.

Eden looked sternly at the gloating RTO. "Try to get Six on the horn and tell him that we're going to take this fucking hill," he told him. He then turned to 3rd Squad's leader. "Keep your people moving, Frantz."

In the open mud terrain, there was no point in forming a line or sending out flank security. They would move up on-line, abreast, with weapons blazing, in the tradition of classic infantry assaults dating back to Napoleon. Frantz pulled himself over the edge of the trench and motioned for his men to follow him up the hill. Before they moved out, however, Motown and Washburn each arched their backs and threw a grenade.

Beletsky in turn wiped the mud off his gold-tipped HE M79 rounds and slapped McDaniel's stubby grenade launcher closed with a loud click. After firing his own symbolic round, he joined the others in an on-line assault on the last visible fortification of Hill 937.

Gaigin and his assistant Bienstock were the closest abreast. Gaigin was laying down covering fire with the M60 and Bienstock was draping the belt of rounds over his forearm to feed it.

"Short burst," the assistant gunner reminded Gaigin, who had yelled the same advice to Duffy too many times to count. "Short."

Gaigin was thinking of Duffy and the M60 bullet he had fired into the head of that NVA when he himself caught a round in the back. It slammed into his spine with a dull thud, like a hammer blow. He was numb rather than in pain.

Bienstock called out "Doc, Doc" and quickly took the M60 and whirled to confront the unseen enemy, but Frantz leaped to his side and pushed the burning barrel toward the ground before he could fire.

It was a sniper, Frantz knew. The guy had waited for them to pass. Now, a retaliatory field of fire would be more likely to hit other men from Bravo Company, who were spread lower on the hill, than any NVA.

With the rest of his men prone and with fingers on their triggers, the squad leader decided to make his own cover and move down alone. He threw a grenade into a cluster of tree stumps fifteen yards away and ran for it as soon as the grenade exploded. He immediately lost his footing, however, and grabbed the first passing stump to keep from sliding all the way back down to the trench. Pausing to catch his breath, he looked back up the slope and saw Doc treating Gaigin. Frantz was certain Gaigin would either buy the farm or never walk again. He once again admired Doc's soothing professional hands and naturally sympathetic facial expression.

As suddenly as Gaigin had gone down, however, Doc too was hit. He lay writhing and screaming but Frantz couldn't tell where the wound was. The sniper was definitely picking his targets carefully. No one would now dare move to either man's aid. The psychological effect of lying in the open mud while listening to the screaming would be just as effective as a company-sized ambush in debilitating the squad's fighting ability, unless the sniper were taken out *fast*.

Frantz scanned the edges of the slope frantically but there was only mud and tree stumps. Finally, he heard the metallic bolt action mechanism of a Russian-made SKS rifle. The sniper was ejecting a shell.

Crawling slowly toward the sound, Frantz noticed an abnormal small mound in the mud, not five feet from him. Moving even slower, stretching and inching his way, he extended his rifle until the muzzle touched the back of the mound. He fired one round, semiautomatic, blowing away the top of the head of the hidden NVA sniper in a shower of heavy mud.

As Terry Frantz again moved up the hill, the rain grew heavier, drops splashing in puddles. The rest of the men were struggling not to slide down backward.

Bienstock, the new machine gunner, was laying down fire in short bursts as the wounded medic tried to revive Gaigin. He called out, "Beletsky, Doc's hit, Doc's hit."

Doc was now shaking Gaigin forcefully, oblivious to the pain of his own wound.

Finally, Beletsky ran from his position and slid to Doc's side. He violently pulled Doc away from Gaigin. "He's dead!" he yelled, with Bienstock still working out with the M60 and the others gazing blankly at the scene.

Beletsky pulled a hypodermic syringe from Doc's own bag and stuck it into the medic's muddy arm. He then stuck the used syringe into Doc's collar, to inform whoever attended him later that he had already had one injection of morphine.

Worcester had now moved up from the platoon's headquarters element and was joining Frantz in motioning and yelling for the men of 3rd Squad to keep moving.

The entire company was sliding and clawing against the mud, with 3rd Squad leading the way. Nearing the final line of bunkers, they could actually see the pith helmets of the enemy who knelt patiently in their trench.

The rain, however, was torrential, bouncing loudly off the Americans' cloth-covered steel pots. Third Squad was so deep in the mud that they could barely make out one another's form. They kept moving relentlessly, like wounded crabs, and the enemy above continued to hold his fire.

The first six men—Frantz, Worcester, Motown, Beletsky, Bienstock, and Washburn—were less than twenty meters from the enemy when the entire slope gave way in a mud slide. Everyone was hurled back, rolling, flopping, or just falling motionlessly. Some grasped helplessly with one hand for tree stumps that weren't there, clutching their mud-clogged weapons in the other hand as they slid past steel pots and bandoliers that others had lost.

Lieutenant Eden and Murphy grasped a stump near the edge of the second trench line and watched in disbelief as the men who had struggled so desperately to take the worthless ground were again denied their objective, this time by the ground itself. Eden picked up the handset but then just let it dangle in his hand. There was nothing to say. Frantz and Beletsky were struggling like child swimmers doing the dog paddle, but could not stop their slide. The others were by now going with the flow.

Three NVA finally stood up boldly from their trench at the crest of the hill and began casually tossing down grenades. Frantz and Beletsky now let themselves slide freely, even praying for a little acceleration, but the first grenade went off right beside them. Frantz was dazed but didn't feel any wounds. Beletsky, however, took a nice slice of shrapnel in his right arm. He finally let loose the grenade launcher with a scream. Terry Frantz tried to ease closer but the earth again gave way. The second mud slide took them both all the way back to the second bunker-and-trench line.

With everyone returned to the initial point of the assault, Platoon Sergeant Worcester pulled himself up, lifting one leg at a time in the heavy mud. The NVA were standing in the open at the top of Hamburger Hill, gloating.

"Goddam," he mumbled, blowing the pelting rain from his lips.

Chapter Seventeen

The rain that had beaten 3rd Squad back from the top of the hill had completely stopped by the time the men returned forlornly to the medevac area. Beletsky and Doc, in a morphine daze, sat next to each other as the rest of the squad strolled and lounged in what had by now become their home base sector of the perimeter. The medevac choppers were still coming in and lifting off at regular intervals, kicking up the usual swirling bits of splintered wood, discarded battle dressings, and tattered clothing.

The thick bandage around Beletsky's arm was soaked with mud as well as blood. Beletsky's legs were folded Indian-style. Beside him, Doc's back was propped up against a stack of wooden ammunition crates. The other medics had pulled Doc's trousers down but had not bothered to remove them all the way. They hung around his ankles as if he were on the toilet.

No one wore underwear in the bush, it only curled and itched. Doc had removed the green towel from his neck and wrapped it around his bare waist and genitals.

Beletsky was gazing intently at nothing as Terry Frantz and Motown approached from 3rd Squad's sector of the perimeter. He and Doc were encircled by other wounded, dead, and dying men. Beletsky's eyes were frozen on the carnage immediately in front of him but he did not seem to realize it. He did not even blink when Frantz stopped at his side.

There was still no reaction as Frantz knelt, lit a cigarette and placed it in the grenadier's lips.

"You got a good one," said the squad leader. "You're going home."

Still no reaction. Frantz calmly walked around to Doc and again knelt, along with Motown.

Doc came out of the daze immediately and dapped with his two friends. Blood was dripping from the six-inch-wide bandage wrapped around his thigh. His fatigue jacket was stiff with mud and dried blood and his wrists were shaking but he smiled as warmly and proudly as if he were being congratulated by two childhood buddies at his own wedding.

Doc knew they were both fighting back the reflexive urge to glance at the wound. Ever the medic, he was determined not to let them get maudlin.

"It's all right, blood," he told Motown. "I don't feel a thing. I am *beaucoup* doped up."

"No, no, Doc. You owe it to yourself," said Frantz.

Blackjack's Charlie-Charlie bird was again circling overhead, flitting and glinting in the sun. Craning his neck and squinting at it, Doc finally began to lose the act. His smile faded to a trembling, angry frown as he watched the bubble-shaped helicopter float so casually above the carnage.

"Blackjack won't be happy 'til he gets every *one* of my people killed," he told the sky.

"How are you going to *act*, Doc?" asked Motown, trying to calm him with the standard GI stoicism. "You're going back to the World."

"I'm just what the World needs," continued Doc, with all pretense of calmness and strength vanished. "Another nigger with a limp."

"Stop that shit," snapped Frantz.

"I'm not 'omitting' you, blood," the freaked-out medic said as he dapped Frantz's palm. "We are *all* no-good dumb niggers on this hill, blood and soul-type." His tone, suddenly, was determined and defiant. "But we *are* going to fool them, aren't we?" he demanded.

"Fucking A," vowed Terry Frantz.

"We've been up that hill ten times and they still don't think we're serious. Who *are* we?" yelled Doc, for all the dead as well as wounded to hear.

Motown was afraid Doc would flip completely out. "Doc," he entreated.

"Who *are* we?" the medic repeated.

"Hundred-and-first!" answered Motown, just as loud.

"Screaming Eagles!" declared Frantz, pointing to his muddy shoulder patch and its intrepid bird.

"Puking buzzards," continued the trembling medic. "Take the hill," he commanded his two buddies, "and those bastards back in the World can never take *that* away from me."

Another medevac bird had cut into the sky, circling lower than Blackjack's loach and then coming in needle-straight and fast for its load of flesh. Frantz and Motown gently wrapped themselves before Doc's chest to protect him from the flying debris thrown up by the rotors' backwash. Beletsky still gazed at nothing.

Leaving their two comrades in the hands of the medics, Frantz and Motown returned to 3rd Squad's sector of the litter-strewn perimeter. Murphy, Languilli, Bienstock, and Washburn had made a C-ration can stove and were brewing a fresh pot of instant coffee.

Without saying anything, as if it were yet another of his normal duties, Frantz leaned toward the heattab fire to take the coffee and fill the discarded green tin cans each man used for a cup. The cup handles were the folded-back lids of the cans.

"Save one for the old man," said Worcester as he watched him pour. He then called to Lieutenant Eden, who was approaching from the command post. "Sir," he called, "can I buy you some coffee?"

The lieutenant joined the circle as easily and naturally as if his silver bars had never existed. "Blackjack wants us to 'maneuver aggressively,' " he announced to the group as he accepted the tiny can of bitter coffee. "I told him *most* of 1st Platoon is still up on that hill." He began trembling almost as badly as Doc had. They were his men, *his* responsibility, regardless of what any other officer wanted done with them and regardless of the fact that not even John Wayne could have taken *this* goddam hill. "We're not going anywhere, Sergeant," he told Worcester defiantly.

"Drink your coffee, sir."

"Why do *you* keep coming back?" demanded the strung-out lieutenant.

Worcester avoided the officer's eyes as he answered, trying to speak as casually as if he were just shooting the shit back at base camp. "Ask me when we're back in the World drinking cold beer and chasing hot women."

"When I get back," affirmed the lieutenant, "I am *never* leaving it again. Flush toilets, hot showers, pizza . . . I want a corn dog with mustard, and

I want some of that good 'free love' I'm always hearing about."

"It's overrated," said Worcester.

"Don't be a lifer," advised Terry Frantz.

Worcester again addressed the junior officer he had broken in so well. "You're right about everybody loving everybody back there, sir. They tattoo it on their foreheads and even wear 'love' buttons on their flowered shirts." Worcester did not realize that he was now the one glaring and trembling with the release of all the pent-up bitterness he had carried up the hill and back. "They love *everybody*. Dogs, cats, niggers, spics, dagos, micks, kikes, greaseballs. And they're *real* fond of Luke the Gook back home. They've got buttons for him too. They'll love everybody but *you*. I was medevacked after Dak To, that was another hill. We were met at Oakland by the prettiest little things, with hair down below their asses and brown paper bags full of . . ." He paused to make the gesture of wiping the dog shit off his chest. " 'Don't mean nothing. Sorry about that,' I says. 'I'm going home. I'm *out* of 'Nam, nothing is ever going to bother me again!' " He had no idea that the others had noticed the tears welling in his eyes. But he was also beyond caring if they did. "The wife is sitting cross-legged on the floor, the kids are running around barefoot, and a hair-head is taking a leak in the john. 'Sorry about that,' I says again. 'Don't mean nothing either.' I go to Paulie's for a beer and Old Man Finnegan is doing shooters. They policed up his boy in the Ia Drang Valley and sent him home in a rubber bag with *members missing* stamped on it. 'Don't mean nothing,' except that he's getting calls from college kids telling him how glad they are that his kid was killed in Vietnam, Republic of, by the heroic 'People's Army' that's sitting on top of this fucking hill. *That's* why I'm here.''

No one dared look into the staff sergeant's eyes.

The silence in the immediate area was still bone-chilling when Beletsky approached them from the medevac area. The grenadier's own eyes were still vacant but he carried his weapon and a full vest of M79 rounds—buckshot canisters as well as high-explosive.

Everyone could tell Beletsky was freaked, and that it wasn't just from the morphine.

Motown was again the one to try to break the tension. ''What's happening, Brother blood?'' he asked Beletsky, trying to hide the concern in his voice but knowing he couldn't.

Beletsky finally stopped walking but continued the suspense, staring up the hill as everyone waited for an answer.

Without even glancing at his surviving buddies, Beletsky started walking back toward the hill. None of the others bothered to finish or throw away their coffee as they picked up their weapons and ammunition to follow him. They fell in line one by one, with no rucksacks, just firepower.

Chapter Eighteen

Everyone in the area took notice of the ragtag file but no one dared ask what in hell they thought they were doing or where in hell they thought they were going. The men of 1st Platoon, the ones who had first encountered the enemy on Hamburger Hill in what was supposed to have been a routine reconnaissance, now had the fire and steel in their eyes that made all others turn away; the fire and steel of men who could no longer be challenged or fazed by anything, even death itself. It was a look one step beyond Open Grave eyes, a look that made even the most senior officers in the area too ashamed to call over to the platoon leader.

They again reached the second tier of trenches and bunkers with no problem, with evening approaching. They then waited for darkness, knowing that the next phase was definitely going to be Indian country.

They split into two elements. With another light drizzle starting to fall, chilling every bone, Terry Frantz took 3rd Squad out to the flank, into the cover of a few trees that had survived all the lead and explosive thrown into the main route of prior assaults. Lieutenant Eden and Platoon Sergeant Worcester then led the rest of the men straight up the same bare slope that had been attempted so many times before, directly toward the next line of trenches and bunkers.

The tactic worked perfectly. The NVA sappers and ambush team sent down from the summit focused all their attention on Eden's group and did not notice Frantz's. Their officer used hand signals to guide his heavy machine-gun team and ambushers into place at the edge of the open area, directly in the line of Terry Frantz's group's silent ascent.

The NVA officer could not believe the Americans' apparent recklessness, crawling up a defoliated slope with a full moon filtering through the clouds and the light rain making quick movement impossible. These were the infamous Screaming Eagles, they were supposed to be among the very best the foreigners had, and they were acting like kamikaze martyrs rather than professional soldiers.

The enemy officer was smiling privately at his prey's stupidity when he sensed something in the bed of tangled, charred tree limbs and bamboo in front of him. He didn't see the enemy's face but recognized the dull curved green wedge of a Claymore mine lying five feet in front of him. He didn't even have time to grimace, however, before the Claymore exploded, throwing a shower of steel balls into his face. The concussion of the explosion sent his body flying back in a half-somersault.

The instant the first Claymore was detonated, Terry Frantz's group set off their other Claymores and threw all the grenades they had as the lieutenant and his men charged forward on the open slope with M16s blazing. One of the GIs popped a parachute-tailed yellow illumination flare to reveal the NVA scampering back up the hill in full retreat, dodging the twisted and melded bodies of their fallen comrades. The sappers dropped their satchel charges and none of their buddies even tried to lay down covering fire.

Terry Frantz and Douglas Worcester both gloated. The NVA were retreating like Boy Scouts rather than the most experienced soldiers in mainland Asia.

As usual, the firing and explosions stopped as abruptly as they had started. Frantz and his men lay in their original flank position and the main element hit the prone on the mud slope. Each group waited for someone else—either the enemy or the other friendlies—to make a first move.

One of the NVA ambushers, still alive but mortally wounded, began crawling, hoping to slink back up to the distant bunkers. His eyes and mouth were straining toward the unseen crest of the hill when a bayonet appeared from the dark and drove smoothly, to the hilt, into his back.

Beletsky didn't bother to wipe the blood from his bayonet, glancing only briefly at the dead man's gaping face before slipping back into the darkness.

Terry Frantz finally crawled to the edge of the open slope and tapped on the side of his steel pot, signaling for his people to follow him on up.

First Platoon moved again in a single indivisible unit, walking on-line despite the moonlight and the fact that they were already low on ammunition. By the time they reached the third line of trenches, the final stopping point before the actual crest of Hill 937, dawn was breaking.

They paused, kneeling among the twisted friendly and hostile corpses, not for a break but merely to reconnoiter their objective before the last push. They were oblivious to the frozen expressions of the dead men at their feet. The only thing they saw, the only thing that still existed for them, was the barely visible final bunker at the very crest of Hamburger Hill.

The enemy hiding in the bunker opened fire before 1st Platoon even moved from the trench, as if to remind them how childish and suicidal they were being. They didn't get the message, however.

Nor did Blackjack, who had been informed of the unauthorized mission and was hovering high above the crest of the hill.

Lieutenant Eden stared numbly at the open ground before him as he listened to the vibrating voice on Murphy's radio.

"Dammit," Blackjack called, "get those men moving. You're being paid to fight this war, not to discuss it."

"Follow me," said Lieutenant Eden, signaling for Murphy, Worcester, Motown, and Washburn to follow him leftward along the trench.

Terry Frantz and the rest of the platoon remained where they were in the trench. Frantz directed everyone to cover both flanks as the lieutenant and his group walked in a crouch over the dead bodies, maneuvering leftward.

"Keep the el-tee covered," Frantz told Bienstock, who had taken over the M60 by default. Beletsky was at Bienstock's side, serving as assistant gunner even though still wearing his vest of M79 rounds. The ground before them was soon piled high with dull gray metal links and shiny brass cartridge shells. He was firing steadily rather than in short bursts. The machine gun's barrel was soon red hot, with the morning mist steaming and silently hissing as it touched it. Darity, the newest FNG, appeared from Beletsky's right with two new cans of machine gun ammunition he had found somewhere in the trench.

As if to again remind the Americans of the futility of their valor, the NVA began popping mortar tubes from the bunker at the crest. The American troops in the trench line pressed against the mud wall, burrowing into both the mud and the dead bodies as the whistling high-angle mortar rounds exploded on-line.

"They're walking them through," acknowledged Frantz as he peered over the edge of the trench. He saw a platoon of NVA trotting down the hill from the right. They were going to counterattack in the wake of the mortar barrage.

"Move the sixty," he told Bienstock, pointing to the right and then glancing at Lieutenant Eden's exposed position on the left. Lieutenant Eden's men were visible targets for the NVA assault troops.

"*Stop* those little people!" Frantz ordered. He then began trotting along the trench, signaling his men to move farther from Lieutenant Eden and concentrate their fire on the attacking NVA.

Bienstock began firing direct support for the lieutenant, zeroing in on the center of the NVA and swiveling the barrel back and forth only slightly.

"That's our goddam people out there!" shouted Languilli as the lieutenant and his men finally charged out of the trench.

"I know that, goddammit!" replied Frantz. "Now *move* the fucking gun!"

A new concentration of enemy fire had erupted from Bienstock and Beletsky's right, where Frantz's group was meeting the counterassault head-on to allow the lieutenant to move forward on the left.

The slower-paced, louder, and deeper noise of a .51 caliber machine gun now joined the enemy's chorus of fire from the crest of the hill. The machine gun was focusing on Eden while the counterassault unit took on Frantz, who was yelling at his men to stay in line and keep moving.

Lieutenant Eden, Worcester, and Murphy were quickly pinned down by the heavy machine gun. The other enemy troops at the crest boldly exposed themselves, as if daring the Americans to take aim, and began rolling grenades down the hill. Two of the lieutenant's men were wounded by the first one.

Eden was on the radio. "Cold Steel, this is One Six, fire mission, over."

He heard the response, "One Six, this is Cold Steel, over."

Then a .51 caliber bullet ripped through Eden's left arm. The next round from the enemy machine gun nest hit Murphy's PRC-25 radio.

Murphy had been in the act of pivoting on his belly to retreat. The monstrous antiaircraft bullet carried fragments of the radio with it through his back and out the open tunnel that had been his chest.

Lieutenant Eden sat calmly at Murphy's side, not even realizing that the enemy machine gun had shifted to the other fleeing troops. The officer held the useless radio's black plastic handset in his right hand and did not seem to care that his left sleeve and arm had been blown away.

"Cold Steel, fire mission!" he called. "Bunker." He began stammering. "Grid coordinates 472, 598 Willie Pee. Fuse quick. I will correct. Say again, I will correct."

Worcester was oblivious to the small arms fire trailing him as he ran back down to the lieutenant's side. He only glanced at Murphy and then pulled a hypodermic syringe from one of his own ammunition pouches. He injected the morphine into Lieutenant Eden's shoulder as the fighting intensified around them.

"Sir." He shook him. "Sir! Your arm. . ."

The lieutenant looked over at what was left of his torn sleeve and finally put the useless handset down. "Oh . . ." was all he said.

Behind the officer, Motown and Washburn were dragging two wounded white men out of the line of fire.

Worcester had the two men put the wounded with the lieutenant. He told Washburn to stay with them, and he and Motown headed up the hill.

As Washburn resumed covering fire, the NVA also began to disappear. The counterattack had apparently been stopped, at least for the moment. Once again, the hill was silent save for the screaming and groaning of the wounded and dying of both sides.

Washburn was kneeling, trying to soothe the wounded he and Motown had dragged back into the trench, when Frantz, Beletsky, Bienstock, and Languilli dove in behind him. A medic was putting a tourniquet on what was left of Eden's arm.

"Jesus—where's Worcester?" demanded Frantz.

"He's up there with Motown." Washburn nodded. The Georgian pulled himself up to go after his friend but Frantz immediately pushed him back into the trench.

"Wait one," the squad leader ordered in a reassuring tone. Frantz then began removing the ammunition and grenades from Washburn's two wounded men.

Languilli set the machine gun down at the edge of the trench. The barrel was warped. "I burned it out." He shrugged, cursing himself for not having followed basic training rules to fire in short bursts. Duffy and Gaigin would have kicked his ass if they had known what he had done to their pig.

With no time for such musing, Languilli picked up one of the wounded men's M16s to follow Terry Frantz back up the hill.

To Frantz's amazement, no one opened fire. He led his men carefully but quickly, single file, all the way to the edge of the final small ring of trenches and the central bunker at the crest of the hill. The sounds of heavy fighting were crackling from the other side of the crest but the section of trench directly in front of them appeared to be deserted. They kept moving cautiously, however, scanning the flanks and rear for snipers or an ambush.

They all froze as Douglas Worcester appeared at the crest, on the other side of the trench.

Worcester was bleeding from several places in the chest and held a bloodied knife in his right hand. He was panting, dazed. Blinking and squinting, he managed to make out Terry Frantz and stumbled toward him. Dropping to his knees, he raised the knife and pointed it to Frantz's left. He then slumped dead with the arm and knife still pointing the direction he wanted Frantz to take.

Third Squad obeyed their platoon sergeant instinctively, with no time to mourn.

They had marched just ten meters to Worcester's left when they encountered the two NVA soldiers he had killed at close quarters with his knife. Without being told, Bienstock, Languilli, and Beletsky fanned out to form a three-point defensive perimeter as Frantz and Washburn kept moving in the leftward direction Worcester had ordered.

Frantz advanced just five feet more and froze again. At his feet, Motown lay dead in a crater filled with punji stakes. A single stake pierced his leg, and his hands were clutched in a death grip around his weapon. Beside him was a dead NVA. It looked like

Motown had slipped into the pit, gotten trapped, then killed the enemy that came to finish him off.

Frantz kept staring, in a morphinelike daze, even as the NVA finally appeared at the crest from the other side of the hill. Everyone else was already lying prone and returning the charging enemy's fire but Frantz was oblivious to the bullets whizzing at his feet. The squad leader had finally reached his limit. Hamburger Hill had finally thrown one shock more than even he could take.

Beletsky finally rushed forward and knocked him down.

"Sarge!" he yelled, shaking him. "Sarge, *Sarge*, we have to get out of here!"

There was still no reaction. The Open Grave eyes still gazed at Motown's wide mouth.

"Ruck up! Ruck up, Sarge!"

The use of the squad leader's own term finally broke the spell. Frantz reached calmly for his weapon.

"We got to get out of here," said Beletsky, praying that Frantz was indeed himself again. Frantz always knew what to do without even thinking, let alone worrying. Beletsky and everyone else in 3rd Squad would follow Frantz anywhere but wouldn't have known *who* to follow or what to do without him.

The squad leader looked back down at the slope they had finally taken, then again at Motown, and then up toward the precise crest of the damned hill, just thirty yards away.

"Don't mean nothing," he muttered as he fired one round at nothing and led his men to the summit.

"Fuck it," echoed Beletsky.

Each man waited for five feet of open ground to form behind the man in front of him before moving up. Washburn fell in behind Beletsky. Languilli, the last man left, reached down to his chest and put his dog tags in his teeth, letting the chain dangle and biting down as he followed his friends up the hill.

The survivors of 1st Platoon stormed the final bunker on-line, screaming madly, with rifles blazing.

Frantz, however, was out of ammo as soon as he landed in the waist-deep ditch. Without thinking, he calmly picked up a dead NVA's AK-47 and nailed two others who appeared from the corner of the trench, five feet away. He was still eyeballing them, making sure they were dead, when another NVA bayoneted him in the back.

Frantz still hadn't comprehended when Languilli rushed to his side and gave the man a vertical butt stroke with his M16. The rifle's plastic stock shattered in the pith-helmeted NVA's face.

None of the men of 3rd Squad had time to glance back and take note of the other troops from other platoons and companies who were finally charging forward from the lower trench line where Lieutenant Eden had begun his assault.

Beletsky was fighting hand to hand with another one at Frantz's left. Out of frustration, the grenadier finally pulled off his steel pot and pounded the man to death with it, fracturing the skull at the forehead as he wielded the steel pot with both hands.

Bienstock was out of the trench and running up and down on the other side of the crest; he was shot, fell to his knees firing the last of his ammo, and died.

Frantz, Beletsky, and Languilli were still taking light small arms fire from the very top of the hill.

There couldn't have been more than two or three left, Frantz was certain. The squad leader was leaning forward to charge again when Languilli doubled over, clutching his belly.

"Alphabet!" cried Frantz.

"Languilli," he corrected as he removed his own blood-soaked hand from his stomach. "*Vincent* Languilli. Remember me. Okay?"

Languilli died before Frantz could answer.

Terry Frantz again fired one round without aiming at anything before crawling the remaining distance to the unmarked, invisible, pointless splotch of burned grass that was the absolute peak of Hill 937. He was soon joined by Washburn, the mellow Georgian, who kept firing down at the retreating NVA while Frantz himself scanned the ground as if in search of a plaque or other marker.

Beletsky hung back to motion the Americans below forward. He had taken command, pointing the angle he wanted each element to take, like a policeman directing traffic back in the World. He was grinning proudly, exaggerating the motions. "Move it, people. Move it! Let's go, people. Move up!"

Beletsky then decided to let the late arrivals find the way on their own, and joined Frantz and Washburn at the summit. Most of the firing had stopped, all of the fleeing NVA were by now out of sight.

Terry Frantz sat in the spot that he calculated to be the exact center of Hamburger Hill, with Washburn and Beletsky collapsed beside him.

Washburn unhooked a canteen from his pistol belt. After a long drink, he handed it to Beletsky.

Watching Beletsky drink, the Georgian could not believe it was the same man who had drained the juice from Motown's tape recorder and called Motown's cassettes "nigger music." He couldn't believe that just two weeks ago, he himself had been an FNG. He had known Beletsky and Frantz forever. They would forever after be part of one another's lives, regardless of what else happened in the 'Nam or back in the World.

Terry Frantz still did not feel the pain of the bayonet wound in his back. Fortunately, it had struck a rib and gone no farther. Turning to watch Beletsky drink, waiting for his own turn, he noticed for the first time that Worrier had strapped a knife and scabbard to the calf of his right leg, just above the boot.

After drinking, Beletsky shook the canteen to see if he could hear the water sloshing.

None of the three exhausted men laughed or commented on the gesture. None of them would ever forget, however, that the sound had sparked the first shot fired on Hamburger Hill.

Beletsky removed the black Skyhawks kerchief from Frantz's neck and poured water on it to wipe the dirt from his sergeant's forehead and cheeks. He then leaned closer and whispered in Frantz's ear.

Washburn raised his eyebrows, trying to figure out what Beletsky had said. He watched curiously as Beletsky removed the knife from its scabbard and walked away. Beletsky held Frantz's scarf in his other hand.

Blackjack's mosquitolike command-and-control helicopter was again circling overhead, lower than it ever had before, as the first small groups of the rest of the battalion reached the top of the hill. Behind these lead elements, others were already carrying wounded back down toward the medevac area.

Most of the men moving back down paused to glance at a crude sign that had been posted on a charred tree trunk. The sign had been cut from a cardboard C-ration box and nailed to the tree with a knife. A black Skyhawks neckerchief had also been

stuck to the tree, below the cardboard. The words
Hamburger Hill had been printed on the cardboard,
in ballpoint pen.

Beletsky stood off to the side of the tree, gazing
down at the bloodstained muddy slope with Open
Grave eyes. He heard a garbled conversation on a
passing PRC-25 radio.

"What is your position, over?"

"Negative contact. Hamburger Hill secured. Say
again. Say again."

"Red One Six, Red Six, over . . .

Red One Six Alpha, over . . .

Red One Six Charley, this is . . .

Red Six, over.

Red One Six Charley, what's your sitrep,
over . . .

Red One Six Charley . . ."

Epilogue

The slapping of the helicopters' rotors and the crackling static of the PRC-25 finally faded as the father glanced over his shoulder and saw his son Vincent approaching. The boy held a tiny American flag that his crying mother had produced from her purse.

Vincent was marching as tall and proud as a Screaming Eagle.

The father rose and himself stood straight and proud, wiping the tears from his eyes. "Over there, Vincent," he told him, pointing to the etched letters that had given his son his first name. "There it is."

As his son knelt to place the flag against the base of the black marble wall, Terry Frantz stepped farther back and saluted the FNG who had been the last man from 3rd Squad, 1st Platoon, Bravo Company, to die on Hamburger Hill.

WILLIAM PELFREY served in an infantry reconnaissance platoon in the tri-border region of Vietnam, Laos, and Cambodia from April 1969 through May 1970. He has since served as a foreign service officer at the U.S. embassies in Pakistan and Venezuela, and worked as a public affairs executive in the oil and automobile industries. His first novel, *The Big V,* won him a National Endowment for the Arts Creative Writing Fellowship in 1973.

by Frank Garrett

WANTED: A world strike force—the last hope of the free world—the ultimate solution to global terrorism!

THE WEAPON: Six desperate and deadly inmates from Death Row led by the invincible Hangman...

THE MISSION: To brutally destroy the terrorist spectre wherever and whenever it may appear...

WORLD WAR II
Edwin P. Hoyt

BOWFIN   69817-X/$3.50 US/$4.95 Can

An action-packed drama of submarine-chasing destroyers.

THE MEN OF THE GAMBIER BAY   55806-8/$3.50 US/$4.75 Can

Based on actual logs and interviews with surviving crew members, of the only U.S. aircraft carrier to be sunk by naval gunfire in World War II.

STORM OVER THE GILBERTS: 63651-4/$3.50 US/$4.50 Can
War in the Central Pacific: 1943

The dramatic reconstruction of the bloody battle over the Japanese-held Gilbert Islands.

TO THE MARIANAS: 65839-9/$3.50 US/$4.95 Can
War in the Central Pacific: 1944

The Allies push toward Tokyo in America's first great amphibious operation of World War II.

CLOSING THE CIRCLE: 67983-8/$3.50 US/$4.95 Can
War in the Pacific: 1945

A behind-the-scenes look at the military and political moves drawn from official American and Japanese sources.

McCAMPBELL'S HEROES   68841-7/$3.95 US/$5.75 Can

A stirring account of the daring fighter pilots, led by Captain David McCampbell, of Air Group Fifteen.

THE SEA WOLVES   75249-2/$3.50 US/$4.95 Can

The true story of Hitler's dreaded U-boats of WW II and the allied forces that fought to stop them.

THE CARRIER WAR   75360-X/$3.50 US/$4.50 Can

The exciting account of the air and sea battles that defeated Japan in the Pacific.

ALL BOOKS ILLUSTRATED
WITH MAPS AND ACTION PHOTOGRAPHS